1/28/19

365

By Marcus Talese

If you could hold the power of god for one year, three hundred and sixty five days, what would you do with it? You have the ability to do anything, have anything, and become anything, tell me what would you do first?

In order to hold god's power there are six rules you cannot break even if you try. However these rules are not the catch to obtaining and holding this power. These rules are, you cannot die even if you try to kill yourself. No matter what you can't leave the earth or even blow up the earth because this means you have left the earth. These are the first three rules you must follow in order to have this gift and use the power of god.

Next is you cannot commit genocide meaning you can't kill off one species. For an example you can't destroy or make all of the fish in the world disappear. This would be unfair. But you can kill several fish and within a second or less you can instantly bring them all back like it never happened.

If someone or another living thing has died before you have been given this power you can't bring them back to life. But the second you are given this power of god you can bring back anything to life.

The last rule is you cannot stop time. Time is inevitable therefore you can't stop it. The clock is always ticking and moving so when the year is up you no longer hold god's power. Now here comes the catch!

After your year is up and the power is gone, you are then reborn again. When you wake up you will not be in the same place you fell asleep at. God's power will place you somewhere else in the world and when you awake you will be naked. This is the same way when you are born coming out of your mother's womb. Also you will never be told where the exact location is of when you wake up!

Not only are you naked when you wake up but you have absolutely nothing. No name, ID, money, clothes, home, vehicle, family members, friends, pets, nothing because you are brand spanking new to the world. There is some good news though. Your debt and criminal history will be completely removed and erased from existence just like it never happened.

Friends and family you once had are still alive. But here's part of the catch. Your friends and family do not know who you are because you never existed until now. Even though you are a day older than yesterday you still never existed to the world until now.

But there is good news, very good news indeed. When you are reborn again you have your memory and physical body but nothing else. Your memory consists of the day you were originally born into this world up until the point you are reborn again. After the time is up the memory and the experiences you had in the past including having god's power will still be fresh in your mind. This means you will never forget what happened in the past.

Enough with the fucking details now it's time to jump down the rabbit's hole head first. You are going to love this I guarantee it!

Chapter 1

A young man by the name of Carl Smith is a college student at Stockton in south New Jersey near Atlantic City. He was majoring in chemistry and bio engineering. Carl is twenty three years old, extremely bright and has only been in trouble twice in his life. However that is not important to this story. Carl was never financially broke and grew up in a middle class home.

Carl wanted to do well for himself and wanted to make more than enough money to support a family. Meaning Carl wanted to make millions if not then billions of dollars. He decided in order to achieve his goals in becoming a multimillion or billionaire, higher education was the key and the answer. Plus Carl wanted to have his own state of the art lab and create new enhancements for both humans and animals.

Carl worked for the first year out of high school in construction. He raised money buy working long hours in construction so he could afford the first year's tuition and have spending money. Carl was driven to do whatever it took in order to become financially successful in life. He had high hopes in learning and obtaining as much knowledge as he could.

Six weeks into attending school at Stockton College Carl met a beautiful bartender at last call which was a local bar. This is a place where mostly college students would hang out at. Carl was nineteen at the time but had a fake ID that looked like the real thing.

This young bartenders name is Leila Taylor. She is twenty one years old with black and blond highlights in her hair. With brown eyes and a great smile, Carl was hooked and drawn to her like a magnet.

They started dating and for the next four years Carl and Leila were a couple. So many great times this couple shared. Concerts, weekends, birthdays and the holidays but the list goes on.

Carl is now at the age of twenty three and is in his fourth year Stockton University. They are still together as a couple but having their ups and downs just like any other. However Carl and Leila love each other very much and tried their best to make it work. Nothing is perfect except for Leila's smile. Her smile got Carl through some stressful times in school. Leila's smile was one of the things Carl loved about her the most ever since the day he met her.

One night after seeing a movie, Carl and Leila go back to her house. Carl parallel parks his truck in front of her house. They both go inside to have a night cap and fall asleep early because Carl had a lot of work to do the next day. However yes indeed they both fucked before falling asleep in each other's arms.

Chapter 2

The following morning it was 55 degrees outside with a light misty rain and medium fog but not too thick. As Carl walks around the front of his truck his notices a flyer on his windshield wiper on the driver side of his truck. The flyer is purple with green writing on it. It's a flyer for a psychic reading and fortune telling.

When Carl grabs the flyer and reads it he quickly looks at the other vehicles around and sees there are no flyers on the other vehicles. Carl thinks to himself why is my truck the only one with a flyer?

Little does Carl know that he has been chosen for something far greater than he can ever imagine! An odd feeling comes over him and he turns around to see a small dark blue house with white windows on it. The house was one story but had a weird and mysterious look to it.

Carl noticed a few things. One he never saw this house last night before on Leila's street. Second the flyer had the same address as this house. But the house had a sign that was painted black with white numbers and letters had the same address.

Carl had an uneasy feeling but at the same time an attraction towards this house. Kind of like an invisible force grabbed a hold of him and was drawling him closer to this house. He checked the time on his watch and it was 7:38 am. "Well I have some time to check this place out before I leave". Carl says to himself as he carefully walks across the street while folding up the flyer and putting it in his cost pocket.

    As Carl walks up a few steps towards this house he looks behind him and sees his black pickup truck is still there and then he proceeds to the front door of the house. Before Carl opens the door he first tries to look into both windows but can't see anything as they are covered from the inside by thick curtains. Carl goes back to the front door with a sign that says open on it. "What have I got to lose "? Carl says to himself and opens the front door.

    When Carl opens the door and walks inside he sees a lot of old books and a bunch of antique furniture. There were a lot of different lamps and unique clocks throughout this home. This place reminded Carl of a combination of two things. An old museum and a ancient library collided all into one!

To Carl's right was an old man sitting in a rocking chair behind a desk smoking a huge pipe. One that looked like Schlock Holmes would use smoke as he thinks about solving the next mystery. While this old man smokes his pipe, a grin starts forming on his face as he looks at Carl.

This old timer had white hair with a white goatee, wearing glasses and wore a two piece suit. This man looked to be between the ages of sixty five and seventy years old. There were no negative vibes coming from this older gentleman that Carl could sense.

"Good morning Carl you made it just in time. I trust you brought that flyer with you". The old man said as he blew out smoke. "Just in time, what do you mean and how do you know my name"? Carl asked with a confused look on his face. "Well Carl, today you have carefully been chosen for a free psychic reading and evaluation. How I know your name is not important as of right now. But not to worry I will explain everything as I go along".

Now Carl was in complete shock and disbelief. He started to second guess himself was this a good idea to walk inside this house? Or should I have torn up the flyer and had gone home? But something told Carl he had to take this chance and see for himself what this house was all about.

"There is no need to be alarmed Carl. Because as you know I'm a psychic, a fortune teller, so therefore I already knew your name before you walked through my door. It makes perfect sense doesn't it". The old man explained to Carl.

"Come on sit down relax and let's talk. Besides I owe you a free reading". The old man said as he walks around to an old fashion bar to grab a fine bottle scotch and two glasses. Meanwhile Carl picks a chair to sit in. Slowly Carl starts looking around the house seeing all of the odd things hanging on the walls, books and other items stacked on the shelves. After the old man was done pouring two drinks he walks over and hands Carl a drink.

"How did you know I like to drink scotch"? Carl asked the old wise man with a smile on his face. "Remember Carl I'm a psychic, it's my job to know these things and many more. So tell me something what do you think of this place"? The old man asked Carl as he began to refill his pipe with cherry flavored tobacco.

"Please follow me Carl and let's sit over here and have a chat". This old wise man says to Carl. They both walk over to where a couple of chairs where. The old man sits across from Carl and next to him was an end table where he put down his drink. There was a small coffee table in front of Carl when he sat down.

"Honestly this place is pretty cool. It reminds me of an old book store that somehow became a museum. It's really retro looking too". Carl said after he takes a sip from his glass. "Why thank you Carl I appreciate the compliments I really do. So Carl I still owe you that free reading just like it said in the flyer". The old man explains to him. "Cool does it include this free double shot of scotch"? Carl asks.

The old man laughs not at Carl but at his comment. The old wise man strikes a match and lights up his pipe with a couple of drags. Afterwards the old man takes a drag from his pipe he puts the burnt match in an ashtray near his drink and says.

"Don't worry about it Carl. These drinks are on me. Now is it alright if I can see the palm of your hands"? The old man asks with a smile on his face. "Sure why not"? Carl said as he puts his drink down on the table in front of him. Carl then sticks his hands out and within five seconds or less the old man reads his palms.

"Ok Carl you can close your hands now". The old man says as he goes back to smoking his pipe. "Really that's all, that quick? I thought you might want to look at my palms longer then that". Carl said with a surprised look on his face. "No that's it; all I needed was a quick glance at your palms. So I see you're in school studying chemistry and one day you want to become a bio engineer". The old man said and then took a sip from his glass. "That's correct, but you know this just by reading the palms in my hands"? Carl responded but this time with confusion on his face.

"I need to ask you something. Who are you really"? Carl asked as he leans forward in his chair. "Well let's just say that I'm a distant friend and the powers that be choose you for something far greater than you can imagine. So therefore the ones who sent me have asked if you would be a good candidate or not. And after I carefully examined you I agreed you are a perfect choice for what we have in store for you". The old man explained with a grin on his face. Then he relights his pipe and smoke fills the air around him.

Now Carl has a mixed feeling of confusion, anxiety, and what's going to happen next? One thought came to Carl and the thought was this. Run now while we still can and there is still a chance to escape. But on the other hand let's see what this crazy old bastard has to offer.

That same old feeling Carl and everyone else in this world have and always think about. The feeling of what if continued to play with Carl's mind. What if this old timer has something good in store for us? Meaning Carl himself and his consciousness kept asking what if this old man is telling the truth. Besides he already knows so much about us. Plus there's a free drink in our hands.

"Who are they? Who are these powers at be"? Carl calmly asked with his hands open. "Well I'll explain the short version of the truth. These powers that be are the infinite universe and multi universes and they are forever all around us, all the time. Who I really am is an extreme fraction of existence within this universe. I am a being of positive energy and I have many names because I've been around for so long. But in this time period my name is Joseph". Joseph explains to Carl

"Carl, trust me when I say that I never needed to look at your palms to read you past, present or your future. I knew your past and present before you walked through my door. The future to come is entirely up to you. But don't worry about anything you are completely safe here. I promise. Joseph says and then takes another sip from his glass.

Carl leans back into his chair and finishes the rest of his drink. As he thinks to himself holy fuck where is this all going? His mind wonders and brain storms as to what the hell is really going on here!

"Ok so what's next? What's the catch here"? Carl asked Joseph. "Carl the catch is one of the greatest opportunities I can ever offer to you. Now also with this great opportunity it comes at a price. However it also depends on which opportunity you choose to take"? Joseph says to him with a smile on his face.

Carl holds his chin and thinks to himself yup here it comes. This motherfucker is going to ask me for money. This is always the catch no matter what the scam is. It's always about money and that is what these con artists want. Carl thinks to himself.

"What I have here Carl is five cards for you to choose from. Each one is very different from the other except the fifth card. The fifth card is very unique and more interesting than the rest". Joseph explains to Carl.

"The first card means you will find the love of your life. This is called the love card. Your soul mate and anything you could ever want in a woman. Beautiful, kind, hard working, intelligent, caring, great mother, and family oriented everything you could ever want in a perfect wife". Joseph says to Carl and then repacks his pipe.

"That sounds like a great deal and I want to believe you completely but I'm going to be honest. I am still a little skeptical about all of this". Carl says to Joseph.

"I understand you being skeptical Carl. But please trust me because here is the catch to this fortune. If you cheat on the woman of your dreams then something extremely bad will happen to you. Your lady of perfection will then murder you and get away with it. Not only will she kill you and get away with it. But most likely she will win big on the lottery! Collect a lot of money and find another man and live happily ever after with him". Joseph says as he begins to laugh.

"Yeah that doesn't sound good at all". Carl says as he sits in his chair waiting for the next offer. "No it's not good at all but these are the rules. As long as you do not break these rules, trust me you will do just fine".

"Now for the second card if you choose this one, is called the money card. If you pick this card you will have more money than you can ever imagine. The actual amount you will receive will be a total of one trillion dollars"!

Carl's eyes lit up like Christmas lights when he heard the amount. "Wow that much money. But I want to ask why a trillion dollars"? Carl said with his hands open and a concern look on his face. "Carl, let's just say we thought it would be plenty for anybody to have and to spend". Joseph says as he strikes a match and relights his pipe. "Ok, well that sounds fair enough to me. But what's the catch for this one"? Carl asked with a smile on his face.

"Let's just say do not become greedy with your money". Joseph says as he blows out smoke. "Becoming greedy will make you evil and money will be the only thing you love and care about. Now I'm not telling you to give away all of your money. And don't give out money to every bum, drug addict, schemer, loser, selfish asshole there is in this world. But choose wisely on who you help with your fortune". Joseph says to Carl as he pours more scotch into his glass.

"I understand and that it makes perfect sense. But tell me something what happens if I do become greedy? What happens next, what's the catch to this one"? Carl asks Joseph. "By the way Carl would you like a refill"? Joseph offers him. "Sure". Carl says as he grabs his glass.

"The catch is when becoming greedy you will wake up one day and no one will be around. You won't have any friends. Your family members will be gone because they will abandon you. Nobody will love, care or even think about you. So therefore you will live forever in your own private hell of selfishness, where your own personal prison is only being about your wants and needs". Joseph explains and then stands up to stretch a little bit.

"The only people who are around you are a bunch of sorry ass sons of bitches. Because they will never love you, care about you, or even like you. These people are only at your side because of your money and what you have. These people will become your own personal demons until the day you die! Most of all you will have no more money because they will have taken it all. That's the catch with this card Carl". Joseph says and then leans back in his chair.

"Fuck, that doesn't sound good at all". Carl says with his eyes wide open. "No Carl it's not, so remember don't be greedy. But at the same time do not become foolish either". "Yes you got that right"! Carl said as Joseph poured Carl another drink.

"Next is the third card. This card is called the life line". Joseph says as he now pours himself a triple shot on ice. "Hold on let me guess this one, I get to live forever". Carl says with confidents. "Good guess kid but no. Nobody gets to live forever Carl. So the life line card is this. You are now twenty three years old. If you pick this card will be twenty three years old for the next two hundred years"! Joseph says as he raises his glass a little bit up in the air. Kind of like a toast in a way.

"You will never age. You won't even age a single day and at the same time you cannot die either. Even if you were hit and blown up by a heat seeking tomahawk missile, you're body will reconstruct itself within seconds. Just like putting humpty dumpty back together again". Joseph says as he snaps his fingers in his right hand and in his left hand holding a drink.

Carl then laughs his ass off. But the thing is this is no laughing matter. Because the down fall and this catch of the life line card is nothing to joke around about.

"Don't laugh to hard Carl". Joseph says with a smile on his face. "This gift will turn you into a weapon and people will worship you like a god.

Therefore you will become a tool or an instrument for militaries of the world! You will cause death and destruction across this planet if you choose to do so"! Now Joseph laughs a little bit and then continues.

"The other curse to this gift is you will see loved ones and friends die while you still live on. Trust me kid this will mess with both your heart and your mind. It will force and drive you deep into the pits of pure madness"! Joseph says as he takes a sip from his glass. Carl then sits there and thinks to myself, holy fuck he is right.

"The fourth card is called the card of knowledge. Now a lot of people will say knowledge is power and they are absolutely right. But too much knowledge can be a horrifying thing to have and to hold! Because when you have all the answers to every question in the world, the knowledge you posses will become overwhelming". Joseph says as he shows Carl the card of knowledge and what it looks like.

This is the first card Joseph has shown Carl but the other cards Carl has no idea what they look like. The knowledge card has a picture on the back of it. The picture is of an old wizard standing holding a crystal ball and inside is the human mind with unlimited thoughts traveling in and out of the crystal ball.

	"Can you tell me how it can become overwhelming? I'm trying to understand in exact detail how it can become overwhelming"? Carl asks Joseph as Joseph strikes another match and relights his pipe.

	"Good question Carl. For example you have the knowledge of knowing who is going to win every sports game including the World Series and the super bowl. You will always know who's going to win because that is a part of the power you posses! This indeed can make you financially a very wealthy man! On the other hand you will have the knowledge of everything else in the world. Meaning you will know everybody's dirty little secrets"!

Carl's eyes opens wide when he heard this and thought to himself holy fuck I'll know what all of the world leaders plans are! "Let me guess I will know what the powers at be are up too at all times? This means the ones who really run this show and control the world. Once they find out that I know everything about them and every political move they make, they will never stop chasing me". Carl says as he stands up from his chair to stretch a little bit.

"That is exactly correct Carl. This is one of several reasons why the forces of this universe have chosen you and so did I. You are quick witted and extremely bright. Throughout the years this universe has only handpicked intelligent people and not a bunch of dumb simple minded assholes. No sir, not at all"! Joseph says to Carl as he prepares the fifth and final card.

"How did you find me and how did you and the forces or the powers of the universe find me"? Carl asked as he sits back down in the chair. "Carl you ask too many of the right questions"! Joseph says as he pours another two shots into Carl's glass. "In time I will answer your questions". Joseph explains.

"Now onto the fifth and last card to choose from called the infinity card". Joseph says as he shows the infinity card to Carl. On the front of this card is a white infinity symbol. In the background behind the symbol is the universe with multiple galaxies all around it.

"Carl this is the card that is extremely unique from all of the rest. It's a lot to explain but I think you will like this one the best. By the way would you care for a cigar Carl"? Joseph offers him. "No thank you Joseph but your right I am very interested in this last card. I'm interested because of the last four you described to me were very intense".

Joseph smiles at Carl as he gets himself ready to explain in full detail what this last card is all about. Little does Carl know but his mind is about to be blown on what he hears next.

"Carl if you decide to accept the infinity card if you choose it. "The possibilities and the power you hold will be endless! There are only a few simple rules to follow and that's it". Joseph explains to Carl with a big old grin on his face

"What do you mean endless? How does that work"? Carl asks Joseph with a confused look on his face. "Carl this means you can have, create and do whatever you want. You can have all of this by simply using the power of your own mind and thoughts. Whatever you think of will manifest itself within a blink of an eye. And your thoughts will become your reality"! Joseph says with his right hand open while holding the pipe in his left hand.

Carl sits way back in his chair with a shocking looking of his face. At the same time he thinks to himself in disbelief this guy is full of shit. Carl's consciousness once again is now being split right down the middle. One part of him wants to thank Joseph for the drinks and leave, but on the other hand a strong of him wants to stay and play the game. For this old man has been right all along.

Carl never told Joseph how old he was and still this wise old man knew his age. A force from Carl's mind and his heart told him to stay and see this through. There was no lying or any bullshit coming from this man. So let's give this a shot and see how far it can take us!

"Honestly it sounds amazing! To hold that kind of power with just a simple thought is beyond incredible". Carl says to Joseph as his interests and curiosity keeps growing by the second.

"You can have anything and I seriously mean anything. You literally possess the awesome, the extreme, the unimaginable and the infinite power of god! However let me explain what these rules are". Joseph says as he strikes another match.

"The first rule is you can never leave this planet. We do not want you causing trouble throughout the entire universe if you choose to do so". Joseph explains

"Second you cannot commit genocide. You can't single out one particular group of people, plants and animals or anything and then destroy all of them. For example let's say you want to eliminate all the palm trees and zebras in the world at the snap of your fingers. We cannot allow you do this because it's to prejudice and to one sided. But you also are not allowed to kill every living thing on this planet".

"The third rule is you cannot blow up the earth. If you did this means you have left the earth. Therefore you have broken the first rule. We cannot have you break the first rule or any of these rules"! Joseph says as he laughs a little and then reaches for his glass.

Carl sits back in his chair listening to Joseph but couldn't move. He was in intense shock. Carl had a look on his face as if he was in a state of a paralyzed panic attack! The reason why Carl felt this way was because he knew Joseph was telling the truth. In some way shape or form he had a feeling this was very real and not some dream.

"The fourth rule is you cannot die. No matter how many times you try to kill yourself, you will still live for three hundred and sixty five days.

One whole complete year you will be alive even if you are blown up by 10,000 nuclear war heads! Even with a tremendous massive explosion such as this, your body will still reattach itself within a matter of seconds like it never happened". Joseph explains to this young man who is in complete shock and at the same time extremely interested.

"How many rules is there Joseph"? Carl asks with a concern look on his face. "Don't worry Carl there are only two more rules left. The fifth rule is you can't bring anything back from the dead before taking and having this power. This means human, plant or animal you cannot bring back. However if a plane crashes into a mountain killing over two hundred people, you can bring those lives back to life. You can bring them all back from the dead within a blink of an eye. This can be accomplished just by using the quickness of your own thoughts". Joseph says with a grin on his face as the smoke comes out of his nostrils.

Carl says nothing still with a shocking look on his face but one thing is for sure Carl is paying attention. He is focusing on not only what Joseph is explaining but teaching him.

"The sixth and last rule is just as important as the first five rules. The next rule is you can't stop time. You can stop objects from moving such as locomotive from running someone over. But time itself will still continue to move along. Because like infinity, time is never ending and it will forever travel into the future to come". Joseph says.

"Dam that is a lot to take in and remember but at the same time this sounds interesting to me. Is it alright if I can have another drink"? Carl asks Joseph.

"Absolutely Carl, as a matter of fact I'll pour you a drink right now. Hang in there I'm almost done explaining the infinite card". Joseph says as he laughs.

"When your time is up and you have lived all three hundred and sixty five days. The next day you will be completely reborn again". Joseph said. "What do you mean by being reborn again"? Carl asked with his right hand open.

"Carl this is the most important rule of all from this card. So please pay attention". Joseph said with a devilish grin on his face as he poured Carl another drink. "After the last minute of the whole entire year is up, you will fall asleep for eight hours straight. When you wake up you will be naked and you will not be in the same place you fell asleep". Joseph explains to Carl.

"What do you mean not in the same place? Where exactly will I wake up at? Hopefully I can wake up in the playboy mansion or even a Las Vegas hotel suite"! Carl asked Joseph and laughs in hopes this could be a possibility.

"Not exactly rookie but I love how you're thinking Carl. But for example let's just say you fall asleep in an upscale condo located in Los Angles California. It's possible you could wake up in a hotel room in Japan or somebody's house in the state of Montana. But to be honest none of us really knows where you will wake up at". Joseph says to Carl as he laughs.

"The other thing you will notice when you wake up is you are completely naked. The clothes you wore the day before will not exist anymore. Your wallet, keys, cell phone, money, ID, social security card and everything else will all be gone as well. But most of all every family member, friend, student and co worker will have no memory of you. This means nobody in the world will know who you are. Your friends and family will still exist just like they always have. However none of them will know who you are". Joseph explains to Carl as Carl's eyes are now wide open!

"The other thing is you will have no identity. You will have no record that you have ever existed. This is a part of truly becoming reborn all over again. Now I want you to pay close attention to this detail very carefully". Joseph says as he takes a drag from his pipe and exhales.

"The only thing you will have left is your memory from your past experiences. This mean from the time you were first born to the time you are reborn again. Whatever you have learned while having the power of god by accepting the infinity card, you will remember the entire experience". Joseph says as he leans back in his chair.

"So when I wake up after the year is over with. What comes next? Carl asks Joseph with a confused look on his face. "You rebuild your life all over again. No, this will not be easy but it has been done before. Trust me you will figure it out and you will know what to do". Joseph says as he shuffles the five cards in his hands.

Then Joseph takes five blank cards and shows Carl they are blank before he puts them in the mix with the other cards. Joseph proceeds to shuffle all ten of the cards in his hands and smiles as he does this.

"Are you ready Carl"? Joseph asks as he gets up from his chair and walks over to a long table. "Let's do this". Carl says without any hesitation. Both of them walk over to this long table and sits down as Joseph starts shuffling these ten cards.

The whole entire time Joseph is mixing the cards around he has this smile on his face. The smile is a dead giveaway that Joseph knows exactly what's going to happen.

"Ok Carl I'm going to mix these cards on the table a little bit more and then you will be ready to pick one". Joseph says and Carl nods his head ok as he looks at the cards being shuffled and waits on the other side of the table. Joseph then spreads the ten cards out on the table but all in a single line. The cards are in perfect alignment and ready for Carl to choose one.

"Carl I want you to take your time and think about which card you want to choose. Think about it and then carefully pick one of these cards". Joseph says with a smile on his face and then reaches for his pipe.

Carl then holds his chin with his right hand as he looks down at all the cards. Carl's eyes glance over the cards back and forth as he thinks to himself, which card do I really want? In his heart and in the back of his mind Carl knows exactly what he wants. Hopefully Carl picks the right one.

Each of these five out of ten cards holds a great deal of power but yet every card comes with its own unique catch. Again Carl starts thinking to himself I can get up and leave right now. But a bigger part of him wanted to stay and take a chance of taking one these cards. To find out and see what it feels like to hold a higher power.

Without hesitation Carl then selects the third card from the right out of the ten cards on the table. Carl holds the card in his right hand and covers the front of the card with his left hand and then he closes his eyes. He imagines and thinks to himself my god whatever card it is I will be grateful no matter which power I possess.

Slowly Carl opens his eyes and uncovers the card with his left hand. He is shocked to see the card is one of the blank ones! "It's ok Carl just pick another card". Joseph says to him. "You knew the card was blank didn't you"? Carl asks Joseph. "You're right Carl and this is one of the reasons why you were chosen. You are a very quick witted man and that's why the universe specifically picked you".

"Please choose another card". Joseph says as he re packs his pipe. Carl looks at all of the cards and picks the last one to the left. Again Carl covers the card with his left hand. Within five seconds he uncovers the card and he opens his eyes wider as his bottom jaw hits the floor. Holy fuck he thinks to himself it's the infinity card! Instantaneously Carl's mind is filled with adrenaline and endorphins as he goes into a state of shock and awe!

Quickly Carl turns the card to show Joseph which card he has picked. Joseph causally looks at the card and smiles with the pipe in his mouth as he slowly exhales the smoke from his mouth like a stoned wizard. You can definitely see the happy and yet proud look in Joseph's eyes as he knows about the ultimate, extreme and awesome power that Carl is about to hold! The infinite card holds an endless amount of god's power just by using your own thoughts. But most of all Joseph knew in his heart Carl was the right individual to possess this amazing power of the infinity card.

"Wow I can't believe I picked exactly this one"! Carl said with excitement as his eyes were still wide open in pure shock! "Carl how do you feel right now"? Joseph asks as he magically makes a new unopened bottle of Blanton's single barrel of bourbon appear on the table. Along with two new glasses made with real crystal! To top it off a clear glass bowl filled with ice with tongs appears right next to the bottle of bourbon.

"Where the hell did this come"? Carl yelled as he jumped out of his chair! "It's ok Carl; everything is going to be alright. Please sit down because I have a lot to discuss and explain to you." Joseph says as he starts putting ice into a glass. Carl slowly sits back down with now a feeling of caution from what he just witnessed.

"Now Carl would you care for another drink"? Carl pauses as he looks around to see if any other surprises are going to pop up. "Yeah I'll have another drink". "Good man Carl that's what I like to hear". "How did you do that"? Carl asks as his curiosity might get the best of him.

"Carl there is several things I can do. But making this fine bottle of booze instantaneously appear is not what's important right now"? Now what is important is whether or not you choose to decide to accept this card? This incredible power the infinite card holds is beyond anything you can ever imagine. Let me explain this you cannot pick another card. This is it kid, it's all or nothing! You can take this unlimited gift I'm offering you. Or you can leave it on the table and walk out the door freely. There will be no hard feelings from me, I promise no bad vibes or anything negative if you decide to leave. So Carl what's it going to be"? Joseph says as he pours a drink for Carl.

	Carl carefully and calmly looks at the infinity card as he holds in his right hand. Carl thinks to himself what the fuck do I have to lose absolutely nothing but everything to gain from an amazing god like experience! In the back of his mind but also deep within his heart both a feeling and a voice cried out.

	Go for it! Take the chance! Ride the wave and ride that motherfucker beyond the limits! Do it, just say yes and take the greatest ride ever known! Live the greatest adventure that was ever told.

Joseph looks at Carl with a mild look on his face as he sits back in chair smoking that old fashioned pipe. Out came the answer that Joseph was waiting for and it's about dam time!

"Yes I want it. I want to take this chance and this opportunity that's in front of me. I will admit that at first I was skeptical. But holy shit you have definitely changed my mind". Carl says as he takes a sip from his glass.

Now I'm going to pause for a minute and explain something. Yes, this is the writer talking to you now. Of course this guy is going to say yes. Did you honestly think I was going to write all of these words and Carl was going to say no! Fuck that, I'm going to push far beyond the limits and the boundaries of the imagination and everything in it! That's right kids I am going balls to the fucking wall with this one.

I'm going to tilt your head back and stretch your bottom jaw ten feet long. Then pour and force two hundred thousand tons of liquid mescaline right down your throat! This will be so unpredictable and thrilling to the point it will make you scream extreme words of madness! This book is going to make Fear and Loathing in Las Vegas look like a can of root beer.

So buckle up, hang the fuck on because the ride of a life time is about to begin. And here we go!

Joseph leans forward as the grin of the joker starts forming in slow motion on his face as he reaches for his glass. "Carl I'm extremely happy to hear you say that! Cheers". Joseph says as his and Carl's glasses touch. "Now you will be number one hundred and one who have been lucky to have and possess this irresistible force known as the infinity card and hold the power of god. This gift is only for the select few and I know and have a feeling you can handle it". Joseph says to Carl.

"Why so many people"? Carl asks with a concern look on his face as his mind wonders for the incredible and the unpredictable to come. "Because as time went on. More and more people were giving the same opportunity as you to experience this gift. But Carl let me get right down to it. Only one man out of a hundred people survived and continued to live his life after the three hundred and sixty five days of containing this infinite power"!

"Only one guy, why is that"? Carl asks Joseph in a state of concern. "Now Carl you already made the decision to accept the infinity card so there is no turning back. If you're having second thoughts on this it's already too late for that. So hang tight rookie this is going to get fucking interesting". Joseph says as he strikes a match to relight his pipe.

"Oh man. Ok let's hear it. I have already heard it all". Carl said with a smile on his face and his hands up in the air. "No you haven't Carl. Not yet you have. Joseph says after he exhales the smoke. "But I'm about to explain what happen to this man. I'm going to tell you the horror this one person created with this power! However I'm going to tell you what happened to this guy when the gift was gone and his time was up".

"The day this poor soul woke up naked in the woods that was located behind a catholic church he was cold, in shock and crying uncontrollably. Until he quickly ran into the church naked, freezing cold and wet, there stood before him right next to the holy water was the priest". Joseph says and then takes a sip of bourbon from his glass.

"Yeah, let me guess he asked for help". Carl said as he reached for his glass. "Oh this man did a lot more than just ask for help Carl! He also cooked, cleaned, handed the priest his slippers, made coffee and even sucked the priest's dick"! Joseph said as his eye brows were standing straight up and laughing his fucking ass off! "Are you serious he did all that"? Carl asked with a shocking look on his face.

"No I'm just fucking around Carl. He did not suck the priest's dick! But one thing is for sure he did make a lot of great coffee for the priest. However this man was forever scared to death about any little thing he did wrong! This happened because of all the shocking and unthinkable things he did while possessing the great infinite power of god"! Joseph said as he shook his head. "Ok, what exactly did this guy do"? Carl asked as he was curious to know how bad it really was. Yet at the same time in the back of Carl's mind he was preparing himself for the unexpected.

"Well I'll tell you about one incident this mad man created. However I have to keep it short because we don't have much time". Joseph says as he pours a little more bourbon into both his and Carl's glass.

"No problem because as incredible this has been I do eventually have to get going and get some things done". Carl says but at the same time Joseph smiles and then drinks his shot of bourbon.

"So this man, well let's call this man John. So one afternoon during his adventure with this power, John decided to walk inside the Millennia mall located in Orlando Florida. This crazy fuck nut chose this place to perform a personal experiment of his". Joseph says as he gets up from his chair and starts walking around the room.

"I'm going to take a wild guess. I think John had himself the biggest orgy with all of the hottest ladies in the world. At the same time everyone was throwing hundred dollar bills at him. And to top it all off he's getting drunk off of free high quality and expensive liquor! Am I right or even getting close"? Carl asks with his left hand open and a confident look on his face hoping he was right. $$$$$$$$$$$

"My god, Carl I love how you think". Joseph then laughs his ass off. "Dam I love how you think! But to answer your question Carl you're not even close. No sir this man had something more sinister and very unique in mind". Joseph says and then re lights his pipe and takes a long drag.

Slowly Joseph sits back down in his chair. "Carl, John was once a good and yet brilliant man who spent most of his time working hard and investing his money. He never took drugs or even indulges in drinking alcoholic beverages. However he was always curious about trying cocaine but never did in fear he would become addicted to that white powder. John's curiosity got the best of him and he wanted to try cocaine for the first time but inside this shopping mall. Now John wanted to do it in a creative and extreme way that would literally blow ever bodies mind"! Joseph says as he smiles.

Carl thinks to himself ok this sounds interesting. In fact Carl was thinking to himself you know cocaine would go perfect with this highly expensive bourbon we have been drinking. Anyways back to John and his crazy idea!

"When John enters the mall he walks to the middle of the mall. He then raises his hands in the air. With John's hands in the air and a huge smile on his face, John then makes everybody stop as if they are frozen in time. Within a quick snap of John's fingers he instantaneously makes every body's heads explode". Joseph says while holding his pipe in his left hand. The eyebrows on Carl's face rise upwards as this horrified him.

"Wait a minute. Why would this guy John want to make people's heads explode when he's trying to do cocaine for the first time"? Carl asked as he was confused about all of this. "Carl, do not worry just hold on, hang in there and relax. I'm going to explain what this crazy asshole did next". Joseph says as he leans forward to strike a match and smoke his pipe.

"Realize this Carl when John made everyone's head exploded inside the mall. This included men, women, young adults, children and yes even little babies". Joseph said in a slightly drunk voice but however still able to keep his composure. Of course at the same time Carl is still in a state of shock and awe! No surprise there.

"After all of the heads are completely off of everyone's bodies, all of the blood comes shooting out of their necks! As the blood of at least one hundred bodies or more starts shooting upward, it all starts collecting in the air like one giant floating blood bath. Joseph explains in a serious. "My god"! Carl says as his bottom jaw hits the table. That's how wide his mouth was open. And then Joseph processes to tell the rest of what happens.

"Now, after all of the blood is finally collected and suspended in midair. John then turns all of the blood into bright blinding snow white pure cocaine! Carefully and yet quickly John separates this massive amount of pure white candy into two gigantic lines. Again with the snap of his fingers and the power of god! John places these two massive lines on the clean marble floor". Joseph says then pauses and takes a sip from his glass.

"Each line is two hundred feet long and two feet wide. Please keep in mind this is more than enough cocaine that could kill over a thousand elephants! John then says to himself ok, how do I go about snorting all of this cocaine all at the same time"? Joseph explains to Carl and takes another sip from his glass.

"By the way Carl I'm terribly sorry for not asking if you would like some tobacco". Joseph asks Carl. "No thank you Joseph. But on a second thought do you have any cannabis"? Carl asks "Indeed I do Carl, indeed I do! Would you like Indica which is highly relaxing and keeps you glued to your seat or a Sativa that gives you a very up lifting, high energy, and positive feeling". Joseph explains. "You know I'll take the sativa". Carl says "Excellent choice Carl I was thinking the same thing". Joseph says as he snaps his fingers.

Magically and within a millisecond a four gram Bob Marley cone sativa joint along with a box of matches appears on the table right in front of Carl. With both hands wide open and a big old grin on his face, Carl takes three wood matches and fires up this monster of a joint.

"By the way Carl would you care to partake in some cocaine"? Joseph offers him. "No thank you sir. After hearing most of the story about John, I think I'm going to hold off on the cocaine for a while. But you know what this weed right here will do just fine".

Carl then takes a drag off the joint and takes a sip of fine bourbon from his glass. After Carl puts down his glass he slowly and comfortably exhales a long twelve second trail of smoke.

"Are you ready to hear what John does next Carl? Joseph asks "Yes sir, let's hear it"! Carl responds back. "Where was I? Oh yes that's right John is figuring out how to snort all of this cocaine and all in one shot. Quickly he thinks and within five seconds his idea not only comes to mind but now it's starting to form". Joseph says as he leans a little forward with his left hand open.

"What do you mean it started to form"? Carl asked with interest in his voice. "Carl John's nose grew four feet long and each nostril became two feet wide! To top it all off John made two straws with a red swirl on them that custom fit each nostril. This motherfucker was ready to drag race that cocaine within an instant"! Joseph says to Carl with intensity in his voice!

"Ok wait a minute how is that even physically possible"? Carl asks with an awkward look on his face. "Carl you have to understand with the infinity card and the power of god anything becomes possible, even physically possible. You just have to follow the six basic rules and not break them". Joseph explains.

"Back to where I was, now John has both straws shoved up his nostrils ready for action. Not quickly but steadily John starts snorting all of this cocaine like a Hoover vacuum cleaner. All within one big long sort it takes John seven minutes or less to finish. After this crazy bastard was done, John breaks off the straws and his nose goes back to normal. The super intense rush racing through his blood stream made John instantly screams with pure power as he felt invincible! Joseph explains and then grabs his glass to take a drink from it.

"John then stretches his arms out in the air and continues to scream like a mad man bouncing off the walls in a padded room wearing a straight jacket! The next thing John does without a second thought he runs at full throttle through the first wall to his right. Like an unstoppable rampaging juggernaut, John continues to run through walls inside the mall". Joseph explains and then sits back in his chair and lights up his pipe.

"God dam"! Carl says after he exhales his chronic smoke. Now with less than half of a joint smoked Carl puts the rest out. His eyes were blood shot red and lit up like Christmas lights! Oh yes Mr. Carl smith was feeling dam good. More like a groovy feeling as the uplifting intense Sativa high mixed well with the bourbon was making him feel more relaxed.

"I know Carl it's insane what this man was doing. And it gets a little more interesting. The final wall John runs through is a solid concert wall that leads to the outside of the mall. However once John was outside of the mall he waves his hand behind him and closes the hole he created. This hole closed perfectly just as if he never ran through it. Like I said before anything becomes possible". Joseph explains and then takes another drag from his pipe. Joseph then offers Carl a refill. Carl Smith accepts the offer and Joseph pours him another double on ice.

"The next thing that happens is John sees this lawyer wearing a suit and tie talking on his cell phone. The lawyer is about to open the door to his 2019 Mercedes Benz 500 AMG until he hears John yelling". Joseph explains to Carl.

"Excuse me sir but I need your help"! John asks the lawyer who is standing in front of him. The lawyer turns to see John and again he asks for help. "How can I help you sir"? The lawyer asks. "Then without warning it happened"! Joseph says with a serious look on his face.

"John kicks the lawyer in his balls so hard it lifts him two feet off the ground. At the same time the lawyer drops his phone and spit goes flying out of his mouth. Before the lawyers feet could touch the ground John grabs him by his throat and with blinding speed John then throws this lawyer twenty five feet in the air and into a tree". Joseph explains with intensity in his voice.

"Holy fuck that is insane"! Carl says with a surprised look on his face. "Well Carl let me explain a little more. John starts laughing his ass off then gets into the lawyer's brand new car all nonchalant. Then he takes off burning rubber and leaving a trail of smoke behind him while moving at ridiculous speeds".

Joseph then tilts his head back and sighs. Meanwhile Carl is in a little bit of shock and awe. Carl relights his joint as he definitely needs a couple of drags after hearing this train wreck of a story. Now Carl is definitely seeing what's in store for him, but also what to expect in the future to come.

"I'm guessing you're telling me this story to prepare me for things I'll be able to do". Carl asks Joseph. "That's exactly right Carl. You also have to remember these six rules because you cannot break them. But let me get back to explaining the story of John". Joseph says as he drinks a little more from his glass.

"John is the only survivor left from having the power of the infinity card. The reason why is because he prayed to god ever hour of every day. Not only that he did whatever the priest and the rest of the staff from the church asked of him. John is still alive today and doing well. However John does this only because he feels guilty for what he has done the previous year. So in order to not to be sent to hell after his life is over, John does whatever he can to make up for the horrible things he did". Joseph explains as he pours another shot of bourbon into his glass.

"What happened to the others? Why are they not alive today? What happened to all of them"? Carl asks as he wanted to know why there was only one survivor left. Because now it's Carl's turn to have this awesome power and there is no turning back now. So yes it makes perfect sense why Carl wants to know what happened!

Joseph makes a sour look on his face and sits back in his chair. "This is not going to be easy to explain. However this will also help prepare you for the end. Meaning when your time is up and the gift is gone you will know what to do. I hope! Joseph says as he crosses his arms.

"Most of them committed suicide, some were also killed and very few died from freak accidents. The ones who died in the freak accidents were because of pure karma from what they have done in their past. To compare all of these people, they were either equal or worse than what John did. "The difference is John was the only one who repent from the unthinkable sins he committed. The instant John woke up naked in the woods, he broke down crying uncontrollably. The weight of the guilt he carried was too heavy for him to handle. This is why Karma did not overcome him in a negative way". Joseph explains to Carl.

"Yeah I can see how this makes sense". Carl says as he takes one last drag before putting out his joint and saves the rest for later. "So this can be my fate is what you are saying"? Carl asks Joseph. "It doesn't have to be Carl I can promise you that. But let me finish telling you about the rest of them". Joseph says to Carl.

"Some of the people who were killed meaning they were murdered still had the same ego, meaning they were about themselves. The only difference was they were now normal just like the rest of the world". Joseph says and then gets up from his chair to stretch again.

"When the gift and the power were gone these people felt as if they were still invincible. The power of god was fresh in their minds and still felt like they could do anything. Joseph says to Carl and continues to explain more.

"Many of them were horribly beaten to death in extremely graphic ways. Their skulls smashed or crushed in. Fingers, legs, eyes, teeth and organs were ripped out and torn from their bodies. All because they had to fuck around with the wrong crowd and again thought they were invincible". Joseph says and then sits back down in his chair.

"Honestly Joseph even though this sounds crazy and messed up. It doesn't surprise me not one bit. I expected worse than what you're telling me now". Carl said without any hesitation. But behind Carl's eyes and into his mind Carl screams to himself. "You stupid fuck! What the hell did you get us into? We had a chance to escape and now we are never going to make it out alive! But yet another part of Carl said to himself. "Fuck it let's take a chance, go balls to the wall and ride the wave of a lifetime"!

"It's sad to say but the ones who committed suicide didn't even last two months. They could not handle having nothing including their own identity. But what really got to these people the most is when they would run into their relatives". Joseph says with sad look on his face.

"For an example a young man from Thailand stumbled and ran into his wife who was married to another man. My god this guy completely lost his mind like you wouldn't believe". Joseph says. "How did he react when he saw his wife"? Carl asked Joseph as he leans forward in his chair.

"He completely lost all control and this drove him into a fit of rage when he saw her with another man. Quickly this man ran up to his wife screaming at her and the new husband reacted by pulling out a gun! Her new husband was an off duty police officer. So the old husband backed down but with tears in his eyes as he looked at his wife. He then turned around and ran off into a crowd and disappearing, kind of like he vanished into thin air". Joseph says as he strikes a match and lights his pipe.

"Carl would you like one last drink with me"? Joseph asks as he reaches for the bottle. "You know what why not, sure I'll take one. But this will be my last drink before I go. Carl says.

"So back to this young man I was telling you about. For years he studied the art of Ninjutsu and Muy Thai kickboxing. At the age of seven years old is when he began his training. Over the years he became a great fighter and this is one of the reasons why we chose him. I'll call this man Lee because I'm not allowed to reveal anybodies real name. But Lee also knew other methods and strategies to use as weapons other than himself". Joseph says as he rubs the sweat from his forehead and takes a sip from his glass.

"Ok what kind of crazy methods would this guy use"? Carl asked. "Primarily Lee would use both chemical and explosive methods for use during war fare. But anyway, Lee was planning his revenge on his wife and her new husband. This only took him about three weeks to accomplish. Lee carefully watched and observed what his wife and the new husband in her life were doing. He planned and timed his surprise attack on her and the husband dam near perfectly". Joseph says as he takes the final sip from his glass.

"Lee carefully prepared a certain drug in a liquid form to inject into her husband. Whoever the person that is injected with this drug will become paralyzed throughout their entire body and it will turn off their central nervous system. So therefore the person will feel absolutely no pain at all! This unique combination can become a deadly method for torturing people as well". Joseph says as he refills his pipe with tobacco.

"So did Lee use this drug on his own wife"? Carl asked Joseph. "Don't worry I'm about to explain that part in a minute". Joseph slowly gets up from his chair to stretch his arms and legs. Joseph then moves his head around to get the kinks out of his neck.

"Now back to where I was. Oh yes, Mr. Lee brings with him the drug I just described on his way to the house where his wife and her husband lives. It only took Lee a few days to find the location of the house. After discovering the house it did not take Lee long to prepare for his unthinkable vengeance"! Joseph explains to Carl.

"This all took place early in the morning around 1:30am when Lee arrives at enters their house. Now with Lee's training he uses the art of being invisible to the naked eye and moves throughout the house in silence. Quickly without making a sound Lee moves through the house unnoticed like it was nothing. As if he wasn't even there that's how much of an expert he was. When Lee finally entered their bedroom he held back a lot of anger! He did not want to wake them up and had to be careful as he injected the drug into his wife's husband". Joseph carefully explains to Carl as smoke came out of his nostrils like a dragon.

"Now as for the wife he had two different drugs for her. One drug to keep her ass asleep and the other to wake her up! When Lee injected the husband with this radical new drug he actually opened his eyes within seconds after the eye of the needle entered into his vein". Even though this man wanted to either scream or fight back, he could not because the drug had already been racing through his blood stream". Joseph explains in detail.

"Wow, now that's definitely a unique way of setting somebody up to be tortured. Not being able to move and at the same time you can't feel any pain". Carl says. "Torture you say Carl. Let me put it to you this way, torture is putting it pretty lightly. Because what Lee has in store for this man is something beyond torture and has never been thought of before". Joseph says as he leans forward while his eyes are open and a grin forms on his face.

"The next thing Lee did was inject his old wife with a drug to keep her asleep while he ties her up. After her hands and feet were tied up Lee then delivered the next drug to wake her up quick! For whatever reason the drug didn't work right away, so Lee started slapping her around until she woke up screaming". Joseph continues to explain further ahead.

"Who are you? Get the fuck out of my house! She screams at Lee but in their native Thai language. I'm your husband, you fucking betrayed me! How could you do this to me? How could you do this to us! Lee screams at her.

"With a confused look on her face, this young lady screamed back. You're crazy; I don't know who you are"! She yells back at Lee still in a state of confusion, horror and shock.

"So what happens next"? Carl asks as he sits up straight in his chair. "The wife looks to her left to sees her husband lying there in bed with his eyes and mouth open. Her husband did not move one fucking muscle other than blinking his eyes. Lee's wife started really freaking out big time"! Joseph explains to Carl.

"Ok so this guy is completely paralyzed, but he is able to blink his eyes"? Carl asks Joseph. "Yes that is correct. I know it's hard to believe but my guess is since blinking is a natural reflex, he was then able to still blink. But anyway, as the wife kept screaming in horror as she looked at her husband Mr. Lee was also still losing his mind! Joseph says and then takes a drag from his pipe.

"Lee then walks to the other side of the bed where he had a custom made Katana sword leaning against the wall". "And now Carl this is where the interesting part starts". Joseph then stands up from his chair and walks around as he still talks to Carl.

"Mr. Lee quickly takes out a Katana sword from its holder and with one swipe from his Katana blade he takes the husbands left foot off. His ex wife starts screaming uncontrollable as the blood starts pouring out of where his foot was cut off. As Mr. Lee's fit of rage continues little by little he starts cutting off sections of this man's arms and legs". Joseph says as he sits back in his chair.

"The last body part Mr. Lee cuts off was this man's dick and balls. Mr. Lee then grabs the husband's dick and nut sack while the wife is still screaming as tears are running down her face. Mr. Lee then walks over to his ex wife and forces it into her mouth. Joseph says as Carl is now and again in a state of shock.

   "As Mr. Lee holds the husband's cock and balls in her mouth he starts screaming at her. Choke on this and die you fucking cunt! This pour woman tries to fight as she moves her head around but eventually she dies from suffocating on her husband's genitals". Joseph says as he sighs with disappointment.

   "I don't get". Carl says. "How did she die from suffocating if she could breathe through her nose"? "I'm sorry Carl. I forgot to mention after Mr. Lee shoved that man's dick down her throat he grabbed a towel to cover both her mouth and nose". Joseph explained.

   "So what happened after she died"? Carl asked. "Well about two minutes later as Mr. Lee stares at his dead wife with tears in his eyes he then takes the katana blade in both hands. Points the blade directly at his heart and without hesitation he thrusts the katana blade into his heart and killing himself instantly". Joseph says as he holds his head and sad because this happened. But Joseph was also sad for the others had died in such horrible ways.

Joseph then sighs and continues to hold his head in his hands. Because he was the person who interviewed all of these selected people who were chosen to hold the power of god from the infinity card. Joseph feels bad and responsible because only one soul out of a hundred is still alive. However John lives in fear for the rest of his life because of the horrifying things he has done and the catastrophic events he created with this power.

Chapter 3

"Carl I hope you are ready for this. I have a great feeling you can be the one". Joseph says as he lifts his head up. "Well, I'm as ready as I'll ever be". Carl says with a smile on his face but also with a concerned look.

"I know you can do it Carl. You can be the one who does things differently this time. But one thing for sure I can promise you, it's going to be one hell of a ride. I guarantee it kid". Joseph says as he puts a smile on his face because he knew Carl was unlike the rest. Joseph had a feeling of certainty this kid was the one to come out on top in the end.

Joseph stands up from his chair and puts his hand out. "Carl I'm sorry friend but our time is up and you need to mentally prepare for what's to come". Joseph says.

Carl then stands up to shake Joseph's hand. "Joseph. Thank you sir, I'm still nervous about everything you have told and shown me. But I am now a believer that this is very real and not a joke. Carl says to Joseph.

"Remember your infinity clock will start tomorrow when you first wake up. Then your adventure will begin. For three hundred and sixty five days you will hold one of the greatest gifts ever known to mankind. You will possess the power of god! Joseph says with intensity in his voice.

"I can't wait to see what that feels like. I believe everything you have told me. And I'm getting myself ready for it"! Carl says to Joseph. "What should I do with the infinity card"? Carl asks Joseph. "Kept it and hold on to it. Trust me you will need it". Joseph answers back as he re lights his pipe.

After Carl and Joseph were done shaking hands and thanking one another Joseph opens the front door for Carl. Carl casually starts walking to his truck. About halfway walking to the truck Carl takes out his keys to unlock the doors.

Carl notices he doesn't feel drunk or even slightly buzzed. This throws him off with a feeling of awkwardness. Then he thought about it for a moment and shrugged it off the best he could. But it still troubled this man and he says to himself. "How the hell am I not drunk anymore"?

Before Carl gets to the door of his truck he stops and turns around to take a look at the house. Carl is now in a state of shock and confusion because the house that was once nice and clean looking is now a boarded up shack. "What the fuck is going on here"? Carl says to himself.

The roof of the house looked like it was going to collapse. Weeds, shrubs, old trees, mold and vines covered the entire house. Each window was boarded up and the steps were cracked and worn covered in bird shit.

My guess is Joseph covered his tracks and he did a good job with doing so. But this gift of great fortune and power Joseph gave to Carl was real. The best of all is this power is unlimited meaning there is no end to the possibilities that awaited Carl.

    There are only two things Carl has to keep in mind. First the six rules Carl have to obey by. Even if he tries to break them he can't. Nothing bad will happen but they cannot be broken no matter what. Second when his time is up having this awesome power everything will be gone. Everything except the memory Carl has since he was born. His memory and physical body will what's left from the life he once had. A new life, a rebirth is what Carl will have until the day he dies.

    "Wait a minute. What the fuck just happened"? Carl said as he takes the purple flyer out of his back pocket. He opens it up and it says the same thing as it did before. Except this time something extra was written on it.

    "Dear Carl, I hope you are reading this message. I have a lot of faith in you will accomplish great things with this infinite power of god you now hold. Hang in there kid and enjoy the ride of a life time, sincerely Joseph".

Carl thought to himself what if it is all real and not just some bullshit magic trick? But the old man did make the bucket of ice; a bottle of bourbon and a joint appear out of nothing. Or maybe it is all real and this card. This infinity card can in fact hold the awesome power of god and I can do, have and become anything I put my mind to.

Carl then takes out the infinity card and stares at it. Slowly it starts to rain as Carl is still looking at the infinity card. But quickly he puts the card away and opens the door to the truck and gets inside.

The infinity card was the same as before. Nothing has changed what was on it. However just like what Joseph said before. It is important for Carl to hang on to it because he will need it later on.

Carl thought about knocking on his girlfriend's door to see what she was doing but Carl had a lot of work to catch up on. Without any rush Carl turns the truck on and puts it in drive.

Then he drives to the college to get some school work done.

Later on that night when Carl finally made it home he thought about what tomorrow was going to bring. Inside that genius mind of his Carl wondered to himself. What it's going to be like to hold this incredible power. Most of all what's the first Carl is going to do with the power of god?

This unlimited and endless amount of infinite power for a twenty three year old human being to have is a major gamble! However this young man was chosen for a reason. Plus Joseph had a good feeling about this kid unlike the others from the past.

It was hard for Carl to go to sleep that night. But before he fell asleep Carl called his girlfriend. Carl said to Leila he loves her and to have a good night. Afterwards Carl lay in his bed while he concentrated and meditated until he fell asleep.

Chapter 4

The next morning, Carl slowly wakes up after hitting his alarm clock on his phone and turning it off. Then he slowly moves his hands to wake himself up. Finally Carl rolls himself out of bed and walks toward the bathroom. Accidently Carl knocks off a bunch of clothes that were hanging from the bathroom door. "Oh fuck it, I'll get after I'm done taking a piss". Carl says as he walks over to the toilet.

After Carl was done taking the first piss of the day he turned around and what he saw shocked the hell out of him. The clothes that were knocked off the bathroom door are now hanging back up exactly how they first were.

"Holy fuck it worked! But how, I didn't ask for my clothes to be hanged back up". Carl says out loud. "Wait a minute that's right I remember what Joseph said to me. You can do anything and become anything with your own thoughts. Wow that man was not joking around"! Carl says as he was still in shock and had his hands on top of his head.

Now it begins! As Carl realizes he now has full control and possess the ultimate power of god from the infinity card. Carl then takes this power for a test drive and really tests it out!

"Ok here we go! Let's see what this power can really do". Carl then closes his eyes and concentrates on what he wants. The house is a mess and Carl definitely needs to clean it up.

He walks to the living room and kitchen area to test out this new power. Quickly Carl closes his eyes and concentrates on what he wants. Twenty seconds later he opens his eyes.

Carl at first could not believe what he was seeing. The entire house was cleaned! Not just one room but every single room was cleaned so well it looked like a new house.

"Well how about that. Fuck, this power really does work"! Carl cries out. Without Carl closing his eyes he had another thought. Then Carl snapped his fingers with his right hand, everything changed within a millisecond.

All of the furniture, TV's, his belongings and every single thing had changed and was different. The kitchen, bedrooms and bathrooms were completely remodeled. All of the furniture was new and upgraded with all brand new hard wood floors throughout the house. The three TV's Carl owned were now all bigger and upgraded with state of the art technology.

"Dam, it works! Yes! It fucking works"! Carl screams out. "I now hold the power of god! Holy fuck I have the power of god! Carl yells holding both fists straight out.

"Ok what to do next"? Carl says and his alarm to his phone goes off letting him he has to get ready for class. "Oh fuck that's right I have to get to class". Carl yells in a state of panic.

Quickly Carl moves his ass and jumps into the shower. But with the power of his mind he instantly makes the water come on and already hot and at the temperature he wants it at. With one second his clothes are off and Carl is inside the shower with the soap and shampoo floating in mid air.

It didn't take Carl long to get cleaned up and his teeth brushed as well. Once Carl stepped out of the shower he was instantly dry as he now had perfect control of his thoughts. Carl walked through the bathroom door and he was fully dressed from head to toe. He was also wearing a five hundred dollar pair of high tech sun glasses and a Movado watch to top it off!

After Carl closes the front door of the house he then snaps his fingers and front door to the house is now locked. At the same time Carl starts his truck before he gets to it. He runs to his truck and gets inside.

Quickly Carl puts the truck in reverse and backs out of the drive way. And then instantly shifts into drive and now he is on his way to quantum physics class.

Within fifteen minutes of Carl driving to his class he runs into a major traffic jam. The traffic jam was caused by a ten car accident and Carl did not have time to waste. So with this amazing power he now thought to himself.

"You know what fuck this I'm just going to teleport to the school. This way I'll have enough time to grab a coffee before class. But where should I teleport to without being seen or noticed? Carl says and thinks to himself.

"I know the bathroom stall right down the hall from class". Carl says as a positive feeling came over his mind. And again with the snap of Carl's fingers within two seconds or less Carl appeared inside the bathroom stall. There was nobody inside the bathroom with him. And Carl remembered to take his bag and other materials he needed for class before he teleported.

With ease Carl makes a large cup of coffee with two creams and four sugars appear in his left hand before he walks out of the bathroom. Carl now has a smile on his face and feels confident that today is going be easy. And why would it not be? Carl now holds the infinite power of god but for only one year.

"How are you doing today Mr. Stein"? Carl says after he walks through the classroom door. Mr. Stein takes a double look at Carl as he is impressed with what he was wearing. "Well your dressing sharp today Carl, what's the occasion"? Mr. Stein asked as he was still amazed that Carl looked like a model from a GQ magazine!

"By the way you're here early today Carl". "Thank you Mr. Stein I was able to beat the traffic today". "Well that's great to hear Carl". Mr. Stein says with a surprised look on his face. Then Carl picks a seat a couple of rows back from the front. Carl kicks his feet up on the chair in front of him after he places his books and whatever else he needed for class on the desk. Carl knows this is going to be to ease as he has a grin of confidence on his face.

After the rest of the students showed up for class Mr. Stein was now ready to teach. But before everyone took their seats some of Carl's classmates were giving him compliments on the suit and watch Carl was wearing. Carl felt positive and good about himself as Mr. Stein started his lecture.

Twenty minutes into the lecture Mr. Stein was asking the students questions about the subject he was lecturing on. Carl raised his hands because he knew not only the answer but all of the answers. And how does Carl know all of the answers? Because of the unlimited power of god, that's how!

Throughout the entire class Carl was able to answer every question Mr. Stein asked. All of Carl's classmates were in shock and impressed by Carl's unlimited knowledge to every question without skipping a beat. When the class was done Carl walked outside of the building with a new boost of confidence and positive mind set.

"Great now what should I do about my truck". Carl said to himself and at the same time Carl's girlfriend just sent him a text message. "Hey babe, what time are you coming over tonight"? Carl text his girlfriend back saying. "I should be there at 9:30 pm. I have a lot of things to get done today. Ok great, I'll see you then. I love you Carl. I love you too baby". Carl replied back.

"Ok now what to do for a ride"? Carl says to himself out loud. Then he thinks about what he really wanted to drive. Carl blinked his eyes and right in front of him was a red all wheel drive twin turbo Saleen S7.

"Dam this is fucking amazing"! Carl said with a smile on his face and opened the car door without touching it. All of Carl's things he had left behind in the old truck he quickly transported back to his house by using his own thoughts.

"Well I don't have to worry about that stuff for now". Carl says as he can visualize all of his belongings inside his house. "You know what fuck going to work. There's no point because I already have the power to do anything and to have everything. Carl says as he is casually driving through the parking lot in his brand new sports car.

"I'm going to go do some shopping". Carl says and then laughs out loud. He pulls out his wallet that has two credit cards in it. Each card has an unlimited amount of credit! Quickly he snaps his fingers and a small duffel bag appeared on the passenger seat filled with five million dollars in cash! With a smile on his face Carl turns up the radio and he drives to the mall.

When Carl enters the mall parking lot he drives through it for less than a minute. Within a spit second Carl instantly transported himself from the car to the inside of the mall without parking the car.

Out of thin air he appears inside the mall with the duffel bag of money. The next thought came to Carl's mind was a pre rolled joint in his mouth already smoking and a glass of ice cold champagne in his other hand. As Carl walked through the mall nobody gave him any bad looks or bitched and complained because he was smoking cannabis and drinking alcohol.

Carl had absolute control as he walked like a boss and a ruler of this world. He was perfecting his power and could control every ones thoughts and emotions. If he wanted to Carl could make everybody in the mall give him all of their money. At the same time Carl could have these beautiful and sexy women in the mall take off their clothes and get on their knees and worship him like a god!

It is truly an indescribable feeling holding this infinite power of god. Carl has now become the king of the world! He just has to obey the six rules and everything else he can do.

Again these rules are one you cannot leave the planet earth. Two you cannot kill yourself. You are immortal for three hundred and sixty five days. Three you cannot stop time. Now Carl can actually stop any living thing or object from moving. However after his time is up using the infinite power of god, whatever he stopped from moving will start moving again. Unless Carl allows it to start moving before his time is up and the power is gone.

Four you cannot commit genocide meaning you cannot kill all the people in Spain if you wanted to. Or kill all of the kangaroos in the world. It would be too unfair and bias but if Carl wanted to kill everybody in the mall by blowing them with a two ton nuclear war head, he could! However after the explosion and the smoke clears Carl can bring all of those people back from the dead. At the same time can fix the entire mall brand new like it never happened within half a second.

The fifth rule is you can't bring back any living being, plant or animal from the past. Only with the time and god's power can Carl bring back the dead.

The sixth and last rule is you can't blow up the planet earth. Even just out of spite or just to see what it would be like. Then put the earth all back together the same way it was. This ability you he is not allowed to have.

And that's it! These are the only few and simple rules Carl has to obey by until his time is up. Everything else is a go. Whatever Carl thinks it becomes reality!

As Carl walked through the mall like he owned the place which he now actually does. In fact Carl now owns the entire world. Again why is this? It is because Carl has possession of god's power.

He finishes his glass of champagne and puts it down on a booth that is selling cell phones. Carl takes one final drag of his joint and makes it disappear. Afterwards Carl snaps his fingers and Sacks fifth Ave appears in front of him. Instead of opening the door Carl walks through the glass to save a little time. Because even with the awesome power he now holds the clock is still ticking and time is against him. But after Carl stepped through the glass he now had a brand new glass of champagne in his left hand.

Carl spends less than an hour trying on new suits, shoes, ties and other clothes he created with his mind. After Carl was done shopping he walks out of the store with his new navy blue suit his stomach starts growling.

Another thought comes to Carl and a table with a white cloth on top appears in front of him. A hot and sexy waitress wearing nothing but a black thong walks over to the table. She brings Carl a plate with a T-bone steak, one whole lobster, and steamed broccoli on it. The waitress also puts on the table not one but three margaritas on the rocks with salt and lime.

One second later Carl is now sitting at the table cutting away at his T-bone steak. Meanwhile Carl's new sexy assistant is breaking apart some lobster claws for him.

"My god I am in heaven right now". Carl says after he finishes his first bite of the steak and then reaches for a piece of lobster. His hot assistant hands Carl a margarita and it tastes better than perfection.

Carl definitely wanted to fuck his new assistant but he promised himself that he would not cheat. Carl wanted to stay faithful to his girlfriend and not jeopardize a great relationship her has with her.

After Carl was done eating and drinking it was time for him to explore more of this awesome power he holds. However before Carl tests more of this ultimate power, he hands his assistant the bag filled with five million in cash. Her eyes were wide open as she screamed with joy. With happiness and excitement this sexy lady starts jumping up and down with her tits bouncing around.

"Have fun beautiful. You have earned it"! Carl says to her and then gives this lady of perfection a kiss on the check goodbye.

"Well I got the teleportation down. Now let's see how well I can fly"? And just like that Carl was floating six feet above the ground giving him a powerful feeling.

The next thought came to mind was to go beyond the speed of sound. Within an instant Carl flew through the roof of the mall creating a loud crashing sound! After Carl literarily shot straight through the roof he instantly reconstructed the roof of the mall like nothing ever happened. Then he flew like superman up into the sky!

Carl flew not only all over town but throughout the entire state of New Jersey. After a little time flew by Carl then made a decision to stop by and surprise his girlfriend. Carl figured he would get there early and show her this amazing power he holds.

Instead of flying through the air to her house Carl took the shortcut and teleported to a bathroom inside her house. Carl wanted to give his girlfriend a shocking surprise as he appears out of nowhere. But before Carl opens the bathroom door his hearing is enhanced by over a hundred times. Carl listens closely and he can hear his girlfriend and other noises coming from her bedroom.

Instantly Carl turns himself invisible and walks through the walls until he reaches her bedroom. What Carl saw not only shocked him but also made him furious. But at the same time this all made sense to him only because he showed up early at 6:30pm instead of 9:30 pm.

Carl's girlfriend was having a 3some with two other guys. One was fucking her mouth while the other was fucking her in the ass! As pissed off Carl was he still kept his cool and stayed invisible. At this point Carl used his eyes to record all of the filthy fun that was going on in his girlfriend's bed. Carl had a plan. After Carl recorded three minutes of her fun it was time to transform back to his visible form again. Carl gave this fucking bitch the surprise of a life time.

"Hi baby, it looks like your having a fucking great time"? Carl yells out but with a devilish smile on his face. "What the fuck"! One of the guys screamed out as the three of them scattered around. "Carl how did you get here"? Leila screamed in total shock and horror.

"What the fuck does it matter how I got here? But that doesn't matter anymore you fucking betraying bitch! Just get back to what the fuck you were doing! You fucking cunt! Carl Screams at the top of his lungs at Leila. Then he starts laughing his ass off. The main reason why is he knows this power he now holds. And by the minute and the second he was learning how to use it.

All three of them were in complete fear and shock because Carl appeared out of thin air! But before anybody could say anything else Carl flew through the ceiling at such incredible speeds. It looked liked Carl vanished into nothing.

"Fuck that stupid cunt"! Carl screamed into the wind but at the same time he was laughing his head off as he flew through the air. This time Carl was over ten thousand feet in the air and fucking loving life!

"You know what I'm not mad. I'm not mad at all. There's no reason to be mad. Because I now have the power! I hold the power of god! Nothing can stop me"! Carl yells out as he is now flying along the beaches of New Jersey.

Carl reaches speeds of over thirty thousand miles per hour and heading south flying over the great Atlantic Ocean. Within little time he arrives in the Florida Keys. As Carl comfortably lands on the beach he is now wearing shorts and a T-shirt with sunglasses, waiting for the sun to set. Carl raises his arms out in the air and tilts his head back and smiles from ear you ear. He does all of this because Carl knows what his next brilliant creation is going to be.

Carl extended the beach in front of him to have enough room for the next best thing. As he put his open hands in front of him a tripped out psychedelic strip club appeared right in the middle of paradise.

There were lights, lasers, strobe lights, fog cannons and neon painted art work all over the outside of the building. The inside of the strip club has the artwork from Alex Grey, Phil Lewis all over the place. Neon glow in the dark paint was used to create their artwork. All of the lasers, fog cannons and the rest of the visual effects from the outside were also being used inside as well.

The tile floor had different tribal designs. The stripper poles were clear and filled with fluid that constantly was changing color. Behind the bar was a lady from India with six arms and huge tits. There were also different chairs and couches to sit on. Before Carl could take one step forward a red carpet with gold lights on each side rolled out to his feet.

    Slowly Carl takes off his sunglasses and places them on top of his forehead. Then the two front doors start to open as Carl crosses his arms. A light red fog or mist comes pouring out from the entrance of the two doors as Carl is greeted by four strippers. Each girl was wearing nothing but a G string and neon body paint. One lady was from Indonesia another from Costa Rica, one was from Sweden, one lady with red hair was from Houston Texas and the last lady was from Brazil.

    These unique and sexy ladies invited Carl inside with open arms and their hug tits were pointing directly at him. Carl rubs his two hands together as he was excited to take a step inside his world and vision of pure heaven! This place was like an excision concert times a million spun out of control!

Countless ladies who are perfect tens were all over inside wearing nothing but g strings and neon body paint with the black lights making glow. Sexy women from all over the globe were inside and each one was Carl's servant.

"Hello Carl what would you like". One lady said who had green eyes and was from Cambodia. Carl took only three seconds to think and then he decided. "Right now ladies I want to candy flip"! Carl says with a big grin on his face.

Candy flipping is a mixture of MDMA and LSD. This was perfect for a world of a psychedelic strip club filled with the best strippers across the planet!

Within ten seconds of taking these two powerful psychedelic drugs Carl was feeling the full power of their peak! My god he was seeing all kinds of tripped out designs, melting effects with different faces and beings.

Two sexy ladies then took Carl by his arms and walked him inside his ultimate dream world. A world that was perfect and fit exactly for Carl Smith. Quickly Carl grabbed both tits on a lady that standing in front of him and she was from New York City. She was half Italian and half Puerto Rican.

Carl sucked the fuck out of her tits like the world was going to end tomorrow! "Mr. Carl would you like a drink sir"? A different lady asked Carl. She was from Paris France and holding the same bottle Joseph had made appeared before. With a smile on Carl's face he said yes and this beautiful lady poured him a triple shot on the rocks.

There were so many different sexy ladies that came up to Carl and each one had a different gift for him! Carl was now in for the ride of his life! One lady had cannabis; another had Psilocybin mushrooms, a short Hawaiian lady had a pouch of American spirit tobacco. Many others had different gift to offer. One girl from Mexico had three tongues with Mayan tribal designs and scorpion tattoos all over her body!

Several ladies escorted Carl to the back of the building where there was a gigantic hot tub. This hot tub was the size of an Olympic swimming pool! There were at least twenty women swimming around naked in this hot tub. Trust me did not take long for Carl to get naked and jump into the enormous hot tub. With a drink in his hand and tripping to its maximum peak Carl has beautiful naked women swimming all around him.

A sexy and voluptuous lady from Greece swam up to Carl. "Hello Mr. Smith, would you like to put your dick between my tits and fuck them"? The young lady asked Carl. "Dam you read my mind and thank you". Carl replied back. Then she took Carl's dick between her tits and started titty fucking him with them.

Three other ladies swam up to Carl as he was getting his dick serviced from this beautiful Greek lady. One girl had a double shot of Marker's Mark on ice him and the second has a blunt for him to smoke. The third was the Mexican girl with three tongues and tattoos all over her body.

Just before Carl was about to cum the Mexican grabbed his dick from the Greek girl's tits and used her three tongues to milk his cum right out of his dick hole. Carl had a smile from ear to ear! While the other three ladies were next to him watching an almost endless amount of semen shooting and covering her face!

"Thank you Joseph for this amazing gift"! Carl said as he laughed and was having the time of his life. This was absolutely the dream vacation Carl had always dreamed of!

Carl was seeing all kinds of insane abstract images, faces, beings, thousands of eyes, serpents with tribal and geometric patterns coming to life all around him. Carl was shocked and amazed at what he was seeing.

Now he was getting his dick sucked again but this time it was two Japanese twins. Carl made them appear instantly from his mind. Both of these girls had long black hair and blue eyes.

Five minute later Carl shot his cum all of the twins. Right behind him was an exotic looking Costa Rican lady with a hose that was attached to a hookah. This hookah was giant and half the size of Carl. This sexy lady packed with the finest Moroccan hash in the world.

Carl spent the next forty eight hours in the greatest creation he has come up with so far. Carl created his happy place, never land, the ultimate heaven he always wanted!

There was so much more to do. With an endless amount of power and very little time, Carl can still do the impossible. He still has the chance to do and complete what the others couldn't. The reason why is because they never thought of it!

Chapter 5

After the forty eight hours were over with Carl, he then decided to return home. But he also knew the fun wasn't over with yet.

It was early in the morning around 5:30am and Carl was looking through his things by having them fly around his house and organizing everything. Carl placed all of his stuff exactly where he wanted them and the next thought came to mind.

He wanted to live in a custom mansion built by his own thoughts and imagination. This would not take Carl too much time complete. But now it was turning 6:00am and Carl's angry and grumpy neighbor next door was about to grab his early morning news paper. So Carl had a little surprise up his sleeve for his neighbor named Doug.

Carl slowly opened his front door and quietly walked outside to the front porch. He was waiting for Doug to come outside and just like always Carl's neighbor was right on time. Directly across from Carl's left Doug walked outside to get his news paper. Carl then decides he is going to surprise Doug like never before. Carl detaches his head from his body and throws his head into the open news paper Doug was reading.

"Good morning asshole"! Carl's head screams out and then starts laughing! "Fuck"! Doug screamed at the top of his lungs! At the same time Doug throws Carl's head up in the air! His head lands on the sidewalk and Doug runs back inside his house.

Carl's headless body starts walking out to the street but twenty seconds later Carl's head re appears on his body laughing. Even though this was only a joke Carl had planned for this to happen all along. But instead this was more of a test to prove that Carl could not die. For he can never die because this is one of the rules he cannot break. No matter what Carl tried.

Steadily Carl is flying straight up in the air and then transforms into a customized military fighter jet. This is the Air Forces new and improved technology and with one sonic boom Carl takes off at blinding speeds.

Carl's next destination is to Amsterdam located in the Netherlands. He has always wanted to visit this city and all that it has to offer. Traveling at the speeds of holy fuck Carl turns this military jet into a flying mansion on the inside. The length of this craft was five thousand feet and two thousand feet wide. This brilliant man had everything you could think of.

Flying in complete comfort and style at sixty thousand feet up in the air Carl was cutting a shave and a haircut. Along with getting his toes nails clipped while relaxing inside a soaker tub with bubbles. His feet were up in the air and his arms were out. And who was doing all of this for Carl? Six hot and exotic ladies wearing nothing but body jewelry made of diamonds and other jewels.

At the bar and kitchen area there was a blonde lady with six midgets helping her to make Carl his breakfast, tequila sunrise, rolling a joint and making peyote juice. The peyote juice was ice cold with lemon and lime slices just the way Carl liked it!

Carl slowed down the speed of the craft because he was having too much fun and did not want to leave just yet. However Carl would arrive in Amsterdam within less than a hour. These seven kind hearted ladies and the midgets served Carl his breakfast, joint and drinks at the same time. After Carl was done eating drinking he lit up his joint and he was ready for Amsterdam.

The hour had already past and the cactus juice was starting to kick in. Instantly Carl dropped and fell through the floor of the craft and flew down straight into the Vincent Van Gogh museum. Without a scratch on Carl or any damage to the museum Carl looks around this amazing museum. Quickly Carl lights a three gram joint without a care in the world and takes a tour of this famous museum.

Now the visuals from the peyote juice were going into full effect as the paintings were moving, melting and expanding. This psychedelic juice was making these paintings expand out and run along the side of the walls. The ceiling and the floor were also moving and grooving to the mescaline trip.

    Mr. Vincent Van Gogh's art work was now coming alive and transforming into a world of Carl's imagination! Meanwhile Carl was walking around taking it all in and drinking champagne with orange juice as he casually smoked his joint.

    Carl walks up to a man wearing a top hat that was looking and admiring a seven foot painting. This was a top hat you would wear to a black tie party. This man was also wearing a two piece suit and smoking a pipe.

    "Excuse me sir are allowed to smoke inside the museum"? Carl asked the man with top hat. "You know something that's a good question. I honestly don't know but this gorilla glue cannabis that I'm smoking is incredibly good". The man said to Carl. "Well my name is Carl". "It's nice to meet you Carl my name is Hector".

    As they both shook hands Carl created two ash trays that stood up for them to use with his thoughts. "Wow how the hell did you do that"? Hector screamed out as he asked Carl. "It's very easy. All I have to do is think about it and my thoughts make it become reality". Carl explained to Hector.

With Carl's next thought he took away Hector's memory from what he just witnessed. Everything was back to normal except now the two ashtrays where still there for them to use. Most of all there was no harm done by taking away a little fragment of Hectors memory.

Carl and Hector talked about different things as the both drank champagne and smoked high quality cannabis. I forgot to mention Carl made four bottles of champagne appear before he changed Hector's two minutes of memory.

After an hour of good conversation went by they both walked around looking at master pieces of Van Gogh's art work. After they were done Carl said goodbye to Hector and vanished into thin air. He reappeared inside the grasshopper coffee shop. Carl was in the smoke lounge but first he wanted to order a triple shot of espresso at the bar like everyone else.

"Wow very cool bong you guys have here"! Carl said as he saw different colors transform into beings and patterns on the walls as the mescaline was going strong. "Do you guys mind if use your bong while I wait for my coffee"? Carl asked as he held the bong in his hand. "Of course you can boss. Go for it". The bartender said.

Carl reached into his back pocket and pulled out a single bud that weighed five grams. This cannabis strain was colored pink, purple and green with a sweet smelling aroma. Cark packed the slide and fired up the bong inhaling the thick smoke. After Carl exhaled the drag he just took his espresso was ready and in front of him.

Casually Carl walks over to a long comfortable lounge chair and it was colored maroon. As Carl stretches out his legs and get comfortable he thinks to himself "What should I do next"?

"I've got it the red light district"! Carl took his time drinking his coffee but he knew time was against him. As Carl relaxed he looked at the painting on the wall of a grasshopper and a naked lady. As this painting changed and morphed into all sorts of things Carl had a smile on his face. Slowly he put on his sunglasses as he took another hit from the bong.

"Well my coffee is done and it's time to take things up a notch"! Carl said as he put the empty cup on a table next to him. Carl snapped his fingers and teleported again without a trace but left the bong behind. He reappeared on one of the streets in the red light district.

Carl saw so many ladies behind several glass doors. But he wanted something different, out of the usual and very extreme rather than what people are use to. Carl closes his eyes and with the power of his mind he brain storms on the next ground breaking idea.

Carl creates a small theater that he was now inside of. The stage was huge and shaped like a half moon. There were several different chairs and couches of all sorts that where everywhere to sit on. The show started to begin after Carl took a seat on a chair with a foot rest at the end.

Two beautiful ladies joined Carl and sat next to him side by side. One lady who was Native American Indian and the other girl was from Jamaica. As the performers came out on stage Carl made a mini bar appear on the side of his chair.

At the same time there was a DJ playing psychedelic trance music on the side of the stage. Three other women walked over to Carl with gifts. The first girl had a hookah filed with Sativa cannabis. Another lady had a six pack of energy drinks. And the third lady had more mescaline juice for Carl to drink.

Even though Carl was already tripping balls he wanted push the limits and make the trip become stronger and last longer. The Native American girl started giving Carl head while the Jamaican girl lit the hookah for him. She would also hand Carl his drinks as well.

The performers were twelve ladies all dressed up in different neon body paint with tattoos and different outfits. There was an assortment of pillows and beds on the stage to put on a show for Carl. Six of these sexy ladies had strap on dildos while the other six girls had several other sex toys to play with. Carl sat back and enjoyed the show as the lights and lasers were going on and mixed well with the visuals from the mescaline.

Once again Carl was indulged with pure bliss and heaven. He watched the girls on stage as they gave each other orgasms with all the crazy toys they had. There was nothing but screaming and moaning on stage while Carl was blowing out purple smoke. At the same time Carl is about ready to blow his load right down the throat of this sexy young lady!

The chair Carl was sitting on transformed into a bed that was custom fitted for him. Before Carl was going to shoot his load the Indian girl was now riding his dick. Then the Jamaican chick hopped on top and was riding his face. After three minutes of this Carl was ready for some air. He signaled and told the girls to get up. Once they did Carl started fucking the Jamaican lady from behind as he watched the show on stage. Carl then un loads his nut sack into her hairless cunt with his arms up in the air screaming!

"Oh fuck yes! Thank you god and again thank you Joseph"! Carl screams out and again with his arms in the air and his dick still in her cunt! Now the mescaline has kicked into high gear and the whole theater became alive. Everything was moving around all over the place to the rhythm of the music playing.

Carl sat back in his custom bed and grabbed the hose to the hookah and took a monster hit of cannabis. When Carl exhaled a huge cloud of blue smoke not only reached out but covered the entire stage as these girls were fucking each with their toys.

With this light blue fog of cannabis smoke blending in with the girls, the cool graphic designs on their bodies were morphing. Their tattoos and neon body paint inner twine with each other and formed into animals, designs, faces, eyes, tongues, beings and slow moving trails all over the place.

The visual hallucinations Carl was seeing were moving along with the psytrance music the DJ was playing. Now this DJ now cranked the volume up to 250,000 watts of pure bass and whole building shook with every bass drop! When this happened the girls on stage started fucking and sucking each other faster with their toys as the heavy bass took over the theater.

One hot blonde girl from Germany was fucking a Puerto Rican who had giant tits with a purple strap on. "That's it you little fucking whore! Scream for me as for me as I jam this purple dick straight into your little fuck hole"! The German lady yells out as her voice echoes throughout the theater.

Meanwhile more women were coming out of nowhere to join Carl and also dance in front of him. Carl was now indulged in a psychedelic, porno graphic, concert. He was impressed with what he created all around him.

Carl stood up from the bed and screamed out "Yes I hold the power of god"! The ladies who were close to him cheered him on and worshiped him like a god! "I remember what Jim Morrison said. I am the lizard king and I can do anything"! Carl said out loud as the music kept playing, the ladies on the stage kept fucking and the girls in front of him kept dancing.

"I'm taking this power to the next step! I want to feel the ultimate power of god! I want the god particle to unleash its true power! Bring me the DMT now"! Carl screamed out with a smile on his face as his eyes were wide open and still tripping hard from the mescaline.

Once again with only a thought Carl created four new ladies and this time they carried out a seven foot hookah! On top of this giant hookah was a hundred grams of pure DMT!

There were two hoses attached to this massive and impressive hookah. Instead of using one hose Carl said out loud "Fuck it I'm using both of them. Girls please help me out". Carl said as the four ladies each climbed their own ladder Carl made appear with big touch lighters.

All at the same time these sexy exotic girls fired up the DMT and Carl inhaled through both hoses taking in the first major hit. After Carl exhaled the smoke everything became more intense and electrifying. Then a female voice from with inside his mind called out take two more! Carl obeyed the command from the voice inside his head and took another monster hit.

More and more intense visuals surrounded him as they became more realistic. Then a humming vibrating sound was coming from within Carl and it was getting louder. Once again the female voice came from inside Carl's head and said "Now take one more hit and come with me". Then Carl took in the final hit of DMT.

Here we go people hang the fuck on! As Carl exhaled the smoke quickly everything started vibrating and shaking like a fucking earthquake.

Then Carl remembered to close his eyes in order to fully launch off. He remembers a friend of his who explained to Carl if he ever tried this medicine to close his eyes.

Once Carl closed his eyes instantaneously his spiritual body blasted off from his physical body and possibly traveling beyond the speed of light! The infinite visions Carl was seeing was a spiraling vortex made from lights, patterns, vibrations and different emotions. Another way to describe it would be the art work of Alex Grey and Phil Lewis coming to life and communicating with him.

"Come with us Carl. Come with us and we will show you the universe"! The same female voice said to Carl but now the voice was all around him. Right after this female voice spoke to him Carl entered into another world. More like another dimension. This was a place where whole cities where moving around like hi tech legos and in the background were geometric patterns constantly forming and shifting.

Several different beings were on the ground and in the air traveling all around Carl. These were spiritual beings, beings of light, physical beings and also dark beings. Some were waving at Carl and welcoming him to their world. Kind of like greeting him in a way as he flies on by.

Without warning the female voice again called out to Carl and said "Come with me and you will see". Carl heard this as he was flying through the air and within half of a second Carl's spiritual form was then pulled back. As Carl was pulled back with such tremendous force he turned around and was launched into another wormhole. A different vortex different than the first but short lived.

One tenth of a second later Carl was inside a dome like place where different colors and designs intertwining with each other. The same voice cried out and said "welcome Carl you have finally made it. We are all happy that you are here. And I am glad you have arrived".

"Who is there? What are you? And who are you? Carl asked as he was in a state of confusion.

He felt an enormous amount of fear but at the same time was curious about the voice he has been hearing.

   A golden yet bright light emerged from with inside the geometric patterns. This golden light started off small but quickly became bigger and more vibrant as positive energy emerged from it. Then this massive light came through the dome in bright golden patterns. This golden light transformed into a spiritual goddess of love, understanding, knowledge, wisdom, the past, the present and the future.

   This spiritual being still had the golden light all around her but also emerging from within her as well. This goddess was the light and the light was her. They were one and the same. She was beautiful and beyond perfection. Different symbols, signs, patterns, and images were constantly traveling through, on and all over the goddess's golden body even including her hair. Most of all this being was larger than life itself and she stood over ten feet tall. However this being can become any size big or small.

Many people have seen, met and talked to her before. She can appear in unlimited forms but for this moment in time and for Carl she chooses this exotic god like female form. She can come in the forms of animals, plants, objects even a forest or a whole world.

If you ever heard of the term god the father then she is what is known as mother. A lot people know her as mother, mother Aya, mother Ayahuasca or Mother Nature.

Carl was in complete shock and awe as he looked at this goddess but at the same he felt nothing but love from this goddess. There was warmth radiating from her that was pure love and understanding.

"Hello Carl how do you feel right now"? The goddess asked him as she could sense the fear within Carl. "Who are you and what is this place"? Carl asked her "I have many names and you are in the fifth dimension. But you can call me mother". The goddess replies to Carl's question. "So you possess the power of god? Don't you Carl"?

Mother asks with a smile on her face. "How do you know this"? Carl asked her with a look of confusion.

Then the ten foot goddess leans down and looks into Carl's eyes. With a grin forming on her face different patterns and symbols moved across her head and entire body. But you could still see her beautiful eyes, nose and smile.

"Carl I am the lizard king! I know everything"! The goddess said with a smile showing her golden teeth. Then she stands up and walks around Carl as she looks down upon him.

"You hold a great power Carl. But you don't know how to use its true potential. Not yet you do. And you are nowhere as powerful as me. But I like you Carl and you know how to have fun". The goddess said as she walked around leaving golden trails from her body movements and long flowing hair. These golden trails were mixing in with different patterns in the background as she walked around.

Carl was looking up at her still in shock but this time without fear. All he could do was watch this incredibly breathe taking ten foot goddess walking around him gracefully. And then Carl pulled himself together and said "Thank you" to the goddess.

"So you cannot die but you cannot leave the earth. This is correct Carl. But Joseph did not tell you everything. Don't worry because I will". The goddess said as she smiled down upon Carl. "Your physical body cannot leave earth. However your spiritual body can travel through infinite worlds, universes, and dimensions". The goddess said and then stopped walking. Now she was standing in front of him. With her hair flowing in a golden light she awaited for Carl to say something.

One second later Carl smiles and then makes himself become ten feet tall. He was now the exact same height as mother. The goddess made of pure golden light says to Carl "nice adjustment". "So do you want to feel and know the full potential of being a god"? The goddess yells out with a smile on her face.

"Yes I want to feel the true power of god"! Carl screams as he is ready to go beyond the limits and boundaries of existence. "Then follow me and I will set you free! But you never will become more powerful than me". The goddess cries out and then the incredible happened.

Carl looked down at his hands and he could see now see his spiritual form. For Carl had now become a spiritual being of light. Carl's spiritual light was blue and he could see the power of god flowing through his entire spiritual body. Carl was amazed, shocked but at the same time now had a new sense of confidence and understanding.

"Now that you can feel its raw and unlimited power, are you ready to leash your true power"! The goddess asked Carl. "Yes I am ready. Show me how. Show how to use the true power of god"! Carl yells as he is ready to learn. "Then follow me and I will set you free". The goddess said as her golden energy started to grow and becoming even more powerful!

Within less than a millisecond they both launched into hyperspace and traveling faster far beyond the speed of light. They both flew through infinite realms, universes and dimensions of existence.

Chapter 6

"Are you getting the hang of this yet Car"? The goddess said as they were flying through multiple worm holes and endless space. The goddess had her arms up over her head in a relaxing position. Meanwhile her golden hair was flowing everywhere. "Yes goddess, this is fucking incredible"! Carl said as he was amazed at what he was experiencing. "Give me your hand Carl". The goddess said as she extended her hand to him while they were both still traveling through hyperspace.

Carl grabs her hand and instantly they both stop. Now they were floating in mid air in a world that Carl has never been to before. This world was similar to earth and another hi tech alien planet combined together.

This planet was filled with mountains, waterfalls, buildings, flying crafts and technology beyond anything you could have ever imagined. The goddess and Carl hovered a hundred feet in the air and they were surrounded by mountains, advanced buildings, flying vehicles and wilderness.

"What do you think of this world Carl? How does it look to you? The goddess asked him as she flew around him with ease. "It's beautiful but what is this place"? Carl asked as he was amazed and impressed at this world around him. "This place is my creation. It's a planet that is only a few minutes old. "But I know every part of this world. And you too have the power to create worlds like this one". The goddess explained to Carl.

From within Carl a new eternal wisdom was growing and it was all around him. Since he was outside of his physical body his knowledge of everything was endless. However Carl still had a lot to learn.

All of existence was endless and the more Carl learned from the goddess the more his power was increasing. Carl knew he could create anything with his mind. However this was his first attempt to create a whole planet within seconds.

Wasting no time and with a smile on Carl's face he snapped his fingers. One second later they were both in a whole new world. It was night time in a city a hundred times the size of Las Vegas. Everything was electrifying as all the buildings were made of light and highly advance technology. This was truly an unbelievable sight to see. The city was connected into one giant electronic life form that pulsated with blinding lights.

"You now see what you can accomplish Carl". The goddess said as she flew and fused into several buildings. "It's exactly what you said before. I am the lizard king I can do everything. Here in the never ending dimensions and mass universes of the spirit world your power has no limits". The goddess said and then she back as a whole being and hovered perfectly in front of Carl.

"However in your physical body on planet earth has a few limits you cannot break even if you tried". She said with a grin as her eyes rolled back. Then this goddess transformed into another female form. With the same golden light illuminating through and all around her, the goddess took the form of Cleopatra the Egyptian goddess.

"Destroy this world Carl! Then build a new one different than the last". The goddess said with a devilish laugh. "You are beautiful mother and far more advanced than I am. But I can't destroy this world, this place. Why would I? I love it here". Carl said to the goddess and now she looked at him with a straight.

"So you are a merciful god. But deep down inside you have a good heart Carl. And I know you will accomplish a great and many wonderful things. I can feel the amazing potential within you". The goddess said as she put her arms around Carl holding him.

"I know this Carl because I know everything. I am what was, what is now and the future to come". The beautiful goddess explained to Carl then she flew backwards not holding him anymore. Two extra arms grew from her body. In her original left hand the goddess created this crystal clear globe. Inside this globe formed a new world and new life forms were created within this world.

"Wow how did you do that"? Carl asked the goddess. "The same way you created the world we are in now. Except this one is smaller. Now watch this and learn from this experience as show what this power can do". The goddess explained to Carl.

This world inside the globe was exploding with fire covering the entire planet. Then the goddess crushed the globe with her hand destroying the small planet as she smiled at Carl.

"Wait, why did you do that"? Carl yelled in absolute horror as he could hear the screams from billions of lives being burned alive. Then the screams stop from their world being flattened into nothing.

"Relax Carl"! The goddess screamed. "Now watch and you will see. You will witness and understand my power". The goddess said as her upper right hand formed another globe and instantly created the same world. Not only was this the same world as before but all of the original beings from the previous world were all there.

"You see Carl; whatever I create I can destroy. But whatever I destroy I can recreate the same as before". The goddess explained in her unique words of wisdom. "Therefore my creations can live without pain or suffering. For the people will not remember their past but only the present and the future. This is one of the true meanings of being a god and to use its divine power". The goddess said as she continued explaining her wisdom to Carl.

"So no matter what bad or evil things we do. We can always change it for the better"? Carl asked. "That is correct Carl. But remember in your physical world you cannot commit genocide or leave your planet. However you still hold an infinite power that you are still learning. Most of all you have a limited amount of time". The goddess explained as Carl listened.

"I want to know more and I need you to show me more. Show me everything you know. Carl asked the goddess with both of his hands open. "I like you Carl. I know you are definitely different from other beings I've encountered. But you alone cannot contain the knowledge of the infinite universes. For you are not ready. Not yet you are". Mother explains to Carl.

"I can see and I know you want to use this power for the greater good. You have an amazing heart inside you and a creative incredible mind". The goddess said to Carl as she now had her hands around his face. Then the goddess kissed Carl long and slow.

"Your time here is running out you beautiful soul. But you will do great things Carl. I know in your heart that you will". The goddess said after she kissed Carl and then looked at him with a smile on her face.

"Wait, what do mean. Why is my time running out here"? Carl asked with confusion on his face. "Remember you hold a great power but you will never be more powerful than me. Most of all you will accomplish great things"! The goddess said as she started growing to over a hundred feet tall.

Within half a second later Carl was launched backwards and into hyperspace without warning. "Wait, wait I have so much to ask you". Carl said as he travels through another vortex at ludicrous speeds. With zillions of eyes of the universe watching Carl travel back into his body, these eyes spiraled around and spoke to Carl in trillions of languages.

Words of wisdom sank into Carl's mind and into his memory permanently. This was only some of the knowledge Carl was asking the goddess known as mother before she sent him on his way.

Then it happened and bang! Carl now shot back into his physical body. Before Carl reentered his physical form, the girls around him were massaging his body and keeping him comfortable. The ladies new Carl was not himself and they knew to comfort him until he returned to his normal self. So these fine young ladies massaged his arms, legs and head.

Carl sat up in his custom bed after he woke up. "I'm back; I'm back in my body. Holy fuck I'm back in my physical body. Carl said as he stood up and started moving around. The girls on stage stopped sucking and fucking each other and were staring at Carl with concerned looks on their faces.

One by one the girls left the stage and the other ladies on the bed walked over to him and asked. "Are you ok Mr. Smith? How do you feel"? Twenty five of the hottest and sexiest women on earth were all around Carl and concerned about him. "Girls I'm fine. Really I'm alright and thank you for worrying about me". Carl said as all of these beautiful ladies now had smiles on their faces looking at him. "What can we do for you Carl"? One of the girls asked Carl and then all of them were asking the same thing. "Girls you have done enough and I thank all of you for all of your amazing talents".

Then it came to Carl's mind these were his creations. He is the king of the world and Carl could do and have anything. Carl listened and remembered what the goddess and the voices of knowledge said to him.

Carl kissed and hugged every lady goodbye. After he was done thanking each one of them Carl made the whole theater shift and transform into the outside of Amsterdam. The theater and the girls were gone. However the ladies did not die or vanish in pain but were no longer a part of existence.

Carl then walked through the streets of Amsterdam as he put on a pair of sunglasses and wearing a new Armani suit. He thought to himself what to do next with a smile on his face. For he knew now what he can do with this awesome power!

Carl casually only walked two blocks down and then he witnessed something traumatic! A five year old little girl ran out into the street without any warning and was hit by a taxi. People were screaming at this horrific accident and the taxi driver came out saying how sorry he was. Over and over again the taxi driver kept explaining in Dutch he was sorry and didn't see her until it was too late.

The poor girl was not only a bloody mess from head to toe but she was also dead from the impact. Her mother held the dead child in her arms screaming and crying. Carl quickly kneels down and says "I can help her. Please trust me". He says to her mother in Dutch. Even though Carl was an American, he could speak any language on earth and throughout the universe.

A blue light was glowing and forming in his eyes as the mother was looking at Carl. A feeling of trust and understanding overcame her and gives the ok to Carl to help her daughter. Carl then carefully puts his hands on the girl's forehead and her heart. Instantly the five year old little girl comes back to life. Not only did she instantly come back to life there was no blood, guts and broken bones on this child. She was so perfect looking it was as if the accident had never happened!

"Thank you! Thank god for you. How did you do that? Who are you"? The mother asked Carl in Dutch. After she asked Carl, he noticed everyone was staring at him in shock. However Carl snapped his fingers and everybody went their separate ways. Their memory was erased and they knew nothing about the accident. Even the taxi wasn't there anymore but in a different location in the city.

Carl took one step forward and before he could follow up with the next step he was already in Egypt. There Carl was standing in front of the pyramids.

The mescaline high Carl was on had faded away a long time ago. Carl reached into his pocket and took out a bag of Psilocybin cubensis mushrooms. Carl thought about how he could help the children of the world. At the same time he started eating these high quality mushrooms as the thoughts and ideas started coming to him.

As Carl kept eating an ounce of these magic mushrooms he stared at the pyramids and thought of two things. One who really made these pyramids and two why were they made? Most of all he wanted to help children. He was proud of himself by bringing that little girl back to life. Carl now wanted to help young kids across the planet that was sick in the hospital. Kids who were also homeless and being abused by adults too.

Carl wanted to use this amazing and incredible gift to help others with it. However at the same time he wanted to have fun with this awesome power he holds. There were so many things he wanted accomplish in the little time Carl had. "Fuck it, I can do both and I can do it all"! Carl says right after he eats the last mushroom.

Carl flew up and hovered around over the pyramids looking at them from all angles. Then the mushrooms started kicking in. The body and visual high was intense from eating the whole ounce. But after his tour of the pyramids Carl took off at blinding speed to St. David's children's hospital located in Austin Texas.

Instantly Carl appeared in the lobby of the hospital after traveling thousands of miles within seconds. People stopped dead in their tracks because this man appeared out of nowhere. But Carl blinked his eyes and everyone went back to their own business like nothing ever happened.

Carl could sense which children needed help the most. Then he made himself invisible. However Carl wasted no time and teleported to the 8th floor and dressed like a doctor.

This child was a young boy at the age of seven years old. His name is Michael Watson and Michael needed a heart transplant immediately. Michael was also suffering from brain cancer and needed surgery.

Little Michael was asleep and Carl was standing at his bed side comforting Michael by transferring his powerful energy. This was to relieve any pain the child was having.

Michael slowly wakes up as he starts to feel better. "How are you feeling kid? My name is Dr. Smith. I'm here to help you". Carl said smiling at Michael. "Where are my mom and dad"? The little boy asked Carl. "Honestly I don't know where they are at now. But I can promise you will be seeing them soon". Carl explained to Michael.

Carl thinks to himself what would be a clever way to cure this child without alarming Michael or anyone else? "I have something for you Michael. Do you like gum"? Carl asked him. "Yeah, I like gum. Do you have any"? Michael asks Dr. Smith. So Carl gave the seven year old kid a piece of gum.

With a single piece of gum was all it took to cure this child from his heart and brain problems. No later than five minutes Michael Watson was cured. There was no need for heart surgery and the brain cancer was completely gone.

As this act of kindness and help was taking place Carl is tripping his fucking balls off! From the ounce of magic mushrooms Carl took earlier he was seeing the whole room shrinking, swelling and transforming into mind blowing visuals. Yet at the same time Carl was able to handle himself in a professional manor. Even little Michael was moving and grooving from the psychedelic visions as Dr. Smith was keeping an eye on him.

"How are you feeling now Michael"? Carl asked him. "I feel great doctor. Can I go home now? I want to go home. I want to see my mom and dad". Michael asked with excitement because he felt a million times better.

"Michael I promise you can go home tomorrow". Carl said as he was writing down notes for the other doctors to read. "You promise I can go home tomorrow"? Michael asked Dr. Smith. "Yes I promise you are going home tomorrow". Carl said as he laughed.

The notes Carl left behind was to inform the doctors of the tests they needed to perform. After the doctors preformed these tests obviously they will find out there is nothing wrong with Michael and release him to his family.

"Michael I want you to do me a favor and get some sleep". Dr. Smith said to Michael. "But I don't want to sleep anymore. I want to go home and see my mom and dad. I feel fine doctor and I want to go home". Michael said as he tried to get out of bed. But within a blink of Carl's eyes he put the boy back to sleep. Michael slowly lied back down in his bed and fell asleep.

Carl vanished in thin air. Yet he left instructions for the other doctors to follow. Another doctor and a nurse walked into Michael's room within ten minutes after Carl left. Where did Carl go you might be wondering? Don't worry I will explain in a minute.

"Who left these notes here"? The nurse asked the doctor after they entered the room. Both the nurse and the doctor read over the notes that were typed rather than hand written. Michael was still asleep as the doctor read over the notes as it explained which tests and scans to perform on Michael. These tests would prove that Carl was cured and could go back home to his parents.

As the doctor continued reading the notes Michael woke up. "Hello Michael how are you feeling today? You look a lot better kid". The doctor said. "Where's Doctor Smith". Michael asked as he was ready to jump out of bed. "Michael who is Doctor Smith"? The nurse asked him. "He gave me this piece of gum and it made me feel better". Michael said to both the doctor and the nurse. "That's good Michael but who is he"? The nurse asked again. "I don't know who he was but he helped me". Michael said. "Well whoever Doctor Smith is he knows what tests to give you". The doctor explained to Michael.

The doctor in the room ordered a medical team to come and take Michael to perform all sorts of tests on him. When the results came back the medical staff was in shock and awe! They could not figure out how this little boy was cured within only a few hours!

The bigger picture here is Carl took the time to help cure a complete stranger. Carl specifically chooses somebody who desperately needed his help. Not just anyone but a seven year old kid. A seven year child who is too young to work, to manage money, to understand things a grown adult would. But most of all, this seven year old child could not defend himself.

These are the reasons why Carl chose not just Michael Watson but any child in this world.

Chapter 7

Carl had vanished from the hospital and teleported to a beautiful beach with perfect weather. Carl was somewhere in the Florida Keys where the water is crystal clear and the sand was perfect. This was truly a tropical paradise Carl was in as he thought to himself how I can help these kids. Not just children in America but every child worldwide.

Carl was in a state of being calm but at the same time he was brain storming. It did not take him long until the answers came to him. "I know what I'm going to do. This should definitely work". Carl says with a boost of confidence. But first Carl wanted to test something out.

"So my physical form can't leave this planet. But my astral body can travel through infinite universes. Well let's see what happens this time". Carl says as he looks up to the sky and smiles. Quickly he takes off from the beach flying straight up. Carl wanted to know if it was true. To find out if it was impossible to leave the earth.

Higher and higher Carl flew towards the top of the earth's atmosphere. Carl was getting closer to the planet's atmosphere. Then quickly without warning this happened. Bang! Carl hit his head just before he was going into outer space.

Carl screamed out "Fuck" after he hit his head on an invisible barrier. "Son of a bitch, Joseph was right I really can't leave this planet". Carl's hands were feeling around this invisible barrier as he tried to find an opening. But of course there was no use and no way off this planet. For this invisible barrier was here to only contain Carl Smith on planet earth

"I really am a prisoner here on earth. Even though I am god for a year I still cannot break any of these rules". Carl slowly yet steadily travels downwards to the same location he was standing on the beach. On the way down to the beach Carl was thinking to himself.

"How can I help the children of the world? With the little time I have left holding this awesome power of god"? Carl said out loud as he was getting close to the beach. Once Carl's feet touched the water and the sand again it only took him three minutes to figure this all out.

"I've got it! I know how this can all work! Holy fuck why didn't I think of this before"! Without even thinking twice Carl disappears in thin air However Carl is not gone. Carl took his power even further and became everything! Mr. Smith now became the earth and the planet earth became him.

"I am the alpha and the omega. I can do anything because I am everything! I am the lizard king and I can fix everything"! Carl spoke and his voice was heard by every living thing across the planet. For Carl Smith has now become the planet earth and the earth was now him.

The earth and Carl was now one living being but Carl also became everything on the earth. The plants, animals, humans, and all of the other objects made of matter Carl became. There's no need to explain how this is possible because with god's power anything you think of is now possible!

With the power of god he cured every child world wide from the ages of birth to eighteen years old. Carl accomplished this by becoming all of the children in the world. Mr. Smith was proud of himself by only using a few thoughts of quickness to complete this mission. Even though Carl saved these kids he went above and beyond that.

Carl took away the pain and the sickness. He also gave wealth and knowledge to the poor. Buildings, roads, parks and even vehicles were rebuilt like new.

With this awesome and amazing power Carl created a world in his own image. A world where everyone was happy and everybody treated each other with kindness. The pollution was gone and the environment was perfect. However nothing lasts forever. But for now the planet earth became a paradise of pure perfection. Carl did the impossible and this was one the reasons why he was chosen to have this amazing power. Even though there's always a chance this man could use god's power for selfish reasons and evil. Instead Carl created heaven on earth!

Chapter 8

With the quickness of Carl's thoughts he changed back into his physical human form. Now he was walking down a cobble stone road somewhere in Ireland. This Carl wanted to walk into a real Irish pub just like everyone else to get drunk. And not use any of his power to walk through walls or just appear inside the pub instantly. He just wanted to have a more than a few pints and hangout with the crowd.

Casually Carl walks into the Irish pub and puts his coat on the chair in front of the bar and sits down. The bar tender walks over to Carl. "What can I get you sir"? "I'll take a pint of Guinness and a shot of bush mills". Carl orders. "No problem sir". The bartender says. "Thank you and I'll be right back". Carl said as he went to go use the restroom.

When Carl returned from the restroom he could see the bartender. There were no drinks in front of Carl and instead of using his power to make the drinks appear. Carl asked the bartender a question. "Excuse me sir, but where are my drinks"?

Before Carl could say anything else the bartender turned around and it was Joseph. "Well hello Carl I see you have been having fun. And along the way you have helped many people in this world. Carl I must say that not only am I impressed but I'm very proud of you". Joseph says with a smile on his face as he places Carl's drinks in front of him.

"Joseph how did you get here"? Carl asks as he reaches out to shake Joseph's hand. Carl had a smile on his face as he was happy to see Joseph. There were so many questions he wanted to ask him.

"Carl, don't worry about how I got here. Trust me; it's not important right now. By the way would you care for a fine Cuban cigar"? Joseph offered Carl as he shook his hand. "You know what I would, thank you Joseph". Carl answered back "Not a problem Carl, here allow me to light that cigar for you". Joseph says and then strikes four matches to light the Cuban for Carl. "So, I hear you met the goddess known as mother. She is beautiful and stunning isn't she? And at the same time, she is unbelievably powerful". Joseph says before he lights his pipe.

"Oh yeah she is without a doubt a powerful goddess! But you never explained to me that I was able to travel outside of this world using my spiritual body by astral projecting from my physical body". Carl says and then takes a sip of Guinness. "Carl to tell you the truth I was not a 100% sure you were going to use DMT. However I'm very happy you decided to smoke the whole hundred grams. I bet the launch from your physical body into the endless realms and dimensions was a mind blowing incredible experience"! Joseph said to Carl with a smile on his face and then took a shot of Jameson whiskey.

Carl has only held this enormous power for a short amount of time and yet with the little time Carl has had he accomplished more than the first one people before him. Without a doubt Carl helped many people throughout the world just by using his thoughts along with god's power. This amazing man definitely put others before himself.

"Yeah that first launch is definitely a nonstop thrill ride! "Honestly I want to go back and experience it again. Carl said and then took his shot of Bush Mills whiskey.

"I want to learn more from the goddess known as mother. Even though I have this ultimate power I could also feel and know she was more powerful than me. But why is this Joseph"? Carl asked as he was curious to know the answer.

"Carl two things, one you can visit the goddess of Mother Nature at any time you want. Second because mother has been around for a very long time. And she was right when the goddess explained. I am the lizard king, I know everything. The knowledge she has is one of several reasons why she will always be more powerful than you". Joseph said as he smiled while he poured himself a pint of Harp.

"How do I become more powerful than this goddess"? Carl asked because he was interested in knowing everything. "That's a great question Carl but the truth is you cannot become more powerful than her". Joseph explained after he took a sip of his beer. "This spiritual being has knowledge far beyond mine. For this goddess is Mother Nature. Because like I said she has been around for a very long time". Joseph again explains to Carl.

"If I do see her again do you think she will tell me everything she knows"? Carl asked Joseph. "Honestly Carl it wouldn't hurt to ask. "Remember you cannot die until your time with this gift is up. On top of that you don't have to feel physical pain either". Joseph explained. "Trust me I know I have already taken off my own head and threw it at the neighbor". Carl said to Joseph as he laughed

"Ah, yes I do remember that Carl. Indeed it was a very clever trick to play on your neighbor. In fact I love your dark sense of humor"! Joseph said as he raised his pint glass in the air. "Wait a minute you saw that too? How did you see me take my own head off and throw it at my neighbor"? Carl asked with a confused expression on his face.

"You have a lot to learn Carl but you will get there. Please understand we are the ones who gave you this gift. I'm not the only one who has been following your every move. Remember how I knew about your visit with the goddess"? Joseph said as he handed Carl another shot of bush mills whiskey.

"That's right you did. So let me guess no matter what I do you know my every move". Carl said with a concern look on his face. "You are learning fast and I know you're the one". Joseph said as he puts his beer on the bar.

Quickly Carl aims a 44 magnum hand gun directly at Joseph's head. Before Carl could squeeze the trigger and blow Joseph's head off within an instant Joseph was sitting next to Carl. Joseph was holding four hand grenades and now both of them were smiling.

"You already saw that coming didn't you"? Carl said. "Indeed I did rookie. But I like the 44 magnum instead of a 9mm. That was some awesome and quick thinking Carl. I fucking love it"! Joseph says to him.

"Who are you really"? Carl asks as he laughs. He thought it was an awesome counter move just like playing a chess game. Joseph then places these four grenades on top of the bar. Within seconds they disappeared. "Let's say I'm your guardian angel Carl. And I'm always looking out for you". Joseph says as he taps Carl on his right shoulder. Carl still laughing makes the gun in his hand disappear.

"No I'm serious what are and who are you really". Carl says as he pulls himself together. Joseph sits there and takes out his Sherlock Homes pipe. "I was born in the year 1645. At the age of twenty three I was a scientist and a dam good one". Joseph says and then takes a long drag from his pipe.

"I was fascinated with astronomy and built a customized telescope. It took me a year to completely make it but back in those days this was a short amount of time. Especially to make something so advanced without any help". Joseph says as he slowly exhales the smoke.

"So you're a ghost"? Carl asks. "In a way yes but I would rather consider myself your personal guardian angel. Like I said before I'm always looking out for you and your best interest". Joseph says as he reaches for his pint glass filled with Harp.

"But Carl I am very impressed with what you have done with this place. You have accomplished what other handpicked people never thought of doing. You have created a dam near perfect world. You created heaven on earth". Joseph says and then drinks half the pint. "You became the earth and put others needs before yourself. This is one of the most generous things I have ever seen anybody do. For that Carl I can never thank you enough". Joseph said as he shook Carl's hand.

"You're welcome Joseph and yeah I wanted to help people especially the kids who could not defend themselves". Carl said as he grabs his pint glass and toasts to saving lives with Joseph. "But look at it this way I still have a lot of time until the year is over with and this gift is gone. I have so many different thoughts on what to do next". Carl said to Joseph. "That's the spirit Carl. I have said it before and I'll say it again. Carl I love how you think". Joseph said and within seconds he vanished into thin air without a sound or a trace.

    Carl still had a smile on his face as he looked at an empty chair that Joseph was sitting in. Carl turned to face the bar and a shot of bush mills whiskey appeared in front of him. Quickly Carl drinks the shot and gets up from his bar stool. Then he takes only two steps and Carl transported himself to the cliffs and mountains of Ireland. Overlooking the ocean and watching the sunset Carl lights up blunt of high powered indica.

    After five minutes passed by as Carl was enjoying the beautiful Ireland scenery. "This is amazing but what should I do now"? Carl says to himself out loud. But also keep this in mind Carl is very stoned right now and feeling relaxed.

Carefully Carl took his time on where he wanted go and what he wanted to do next. Now Carl is floating over the cliffs of Ireland still smoking his blunt. Then his next thought was Las Vegas Nevada! Las Vegas is one city Carl always wanted to visit but never had the time or the money to go.

But now is a completely different story. As Carl was still floating around off the cliffs of Ireland he takes one last drag from his blunt. Afterwards he lightly throws the blunt up in the air and snaps his fingers, within a second the blunt disappears. With a devilish grin on Carl face he exhales a massive cloud of cannabis smoke and launches at ten thousand miles per hour heading west!

Carl decided to fly this time rather than teleport to Las Vegas. When he finally arrived in the city of Las Vegas it was better than ever and beyond perfection. Carl transformed this city bigger and better than it was before. Everything about this city was built to perfection and crime was very little to none at all.

It was night time in Las Vegas Nevada when Carl arrived. Floating twelve hundred feet in the air Carl looked down and around seeing all of the beautiful lights and buildings. This is one of the reasons why he wanted to visit Vegas for all that it has to offer!

"Man this is amazing. Even though I made the earth into a perfect world I'm also happy I transformed this city into something better. This looks like a perfect night for psychedelic medication and another mind blowing adventure"! Carl says as he kept looking down at the city below.

In front of Carl a clear liquid mass was forming and becoming bigger. Eventually this liquid mass became the exact size of Carl. With a blink of an eye Carl's clothes along with his watch disappeared and he was completely naked. This liquid mass then attached to him covering his entire body. Quickly this liquid substance entered Carl's body through his pours, even including his eyes.

Thank god Carl is able to turn off his central nervous system so he could not feel any pain. Or this liquid LSD would have burned as it entered through his eyes and other parts of his body. Yes indeed LSD is what was running through every inch of Carl's body. After the process was fully complete Carl became twice his normal size. This means he was twelve feet tall!

Other than the DMT trip Carl experienced when he was completely blown while meeting the goddess, this next LSD trip is the second most extreme psychedelic journey! It took only less than a minute for the acid to kick into high gear. Waving his arms around Carl was seeing all sorts of trails!

"HA HA" Carl starts laughing like a madman! However he has complete control of himself and magnifies the LSD with the infinite power of god. There were no fear, no pain, and no worry in the world as Carl smiles and again looks down at the city below him. This man was definitely ready for a night out in Las Vegas!

Carl closes his eyes and vanishes but reappears on a stage during a live show where a magician was performing. The crowd was in shock and awe as they saw this twelve foot naked man. Quickly Carl transformed back into his usual size at six feet tall. But now Carl is wearing a two piece suite with a giant black top hat.

The audience and magician were still in shock and disbelief from what they were witnessing! For this was no magic trick being performed, this was real life!

"It's ok please relax it's only a trick I promise". Carl says to everyone including the magician himself. Then Carl takes off his hat and turns it over. Slowly Carl reaches into the hat and pulls out a cute puppy. A golden retriever puppy! The people in the audience were applauding with smiles on their faces.

Once Carl put this puppy on the floor it started multiplying rapidly as the puppy walked across the stage. One puppy after the other appeared as the first one kept walking across the stage. More clones were made and within a minute twenty five puppy clones were on stage. The audience was excited and happy with joy to see this! Carl was also happy because he created something good and positive.

But yes, yes Carl was peaking extremely hard and the pupils in his eyes were black like the dark abyss. Indeed Carl was tripping fucking hard! He was seeing and feeling all kinds of insane visuals. Everything was coming alive! Multiple beings, geometric patterns, intense melting with abstract visions were all fusing into one another. The venue was in a never ending transformation of psychedelic madness!

At the same time all twenty five of the puppies jumped off the stage and ran up to all of the people in the audience. These excited puppies were licking everybody and waging their tales. They were spreading unconditional love and happiness to the audience. This was the plan Carl had all along when he pulled the first puppy out of his top hat!

"How did you that"? The magician asked Carl. "It's magic. Just good old fashioned magic, that's all". Carl explained as he saw the magician's face was melting, moving, and shifting in different tribal designs.

"I've never seen magic this before". The magician said with awe struck confusing look on his face. "Don't worry. It's because this type of magic has never been done before". Carl Smith replied back to the magician. "Are you ready for my next trick? You're going to love this one I guarantee it". Carl says.

A giant grin formed on Carl's face as he held his hat. Carl then threw the hat towards the audience. The hat was standing upright and flying through the air. While the hat flew through the air from the bottom of the hat $100 dollar bills shot out of underneath and into the audience. Over one hundred million dollars was shooting out of the hat extremely fast!

Everyone in the audience stood up from their seats with their hands up in the air catching every

$100 bill they could. What you heard in the audience as people were trying to gather all this free money was laughing, screaming and yelling.

Within a short amount of time the worst happened. Even though Carl created heaven on earth the evil of human beings was now unleashed inside this venue. Now people were fighting over this free money falling on top of them. These sons of bitches were so consumed by their own horrible greed they forgot about all the cute puppies.

You could see the sin of greed in the eyes of these self centered bastards like a fucking sickness without a cure. As Carl watched this shit storm unfold the people in the audience were punching, strangling, pulling hair, grabbing, scratching, pushing and kicking each other. Of course this not what Carl wanted or what he was expecting.

"That's it"! Carl screamed out into the crowd in an extremely loud voice. The crowd stopped and paused as they all now looked at Carl. With the quickness of Carl's next thought he instantly made all of the money disappear!

Please keep in mind that the massive amount of pure LSD running through Carl's veins has now shifted into a higher gear. As this extreme psychedelic drug was running at full throttle Carl saw these people transform into these ugly looking demons. Their faces and body's shift and changed into horrific demonic entities!

Now all of the attention was directed towards Carl and the audience was screaming and yelling at him. The crowd was calling Carl all kinds of insane names and other evil things. Then quickly all the people in the audience ran towards Carl to try and kill him. They were fucking pissed off with an uncontrollable fit of rage! All because Carl took away the money in order to stop the violence and the greed from continuing.

Carl stood his ground with a smile on his face. And just before these demons reached him, Carl blinked his eyes. Without a sound the demons were all sitting back in their seats smiling back at Carl.

Now any normal person tripping as hard as Carl was would have lost their minds and panicked. However when you have the power of god and full control of it then you have nothing to fear. Because once again you can control everything!

"So how are we doing tonight"? Carl asked the audience who were still these ugly horrifying demons but still smiling at Carl. "Come on let me hear you". And with the snap of his fingers Carl transformed the demons back into their normal human being selves. Right after the transformation was complete the audience stood up and cheered Carl on. "Thank you and all of have been great". Carl said then vanished into the air again.

Chapter 9

This man with great and awesome power wasted no time in doing exactly what he wanted. Carl reappeared inside of a building that was half a casino and half a whore house. The name of this upscale fine establishment was called gold diggers! I personally think it's a rather catchy name.

Carl is now wearing a new suite with a Movado watch as he walks towards the poker table. Texas hold'em is the game Carl wanted to play. Carl put a million dollars worth of chips on the table before he sat down and the five other players at the table were in shock! The five players looked at Carl like who the fuck is this high roller?

The dealer quickly handed out two cards for each player. Carl had a king and queen of hearts. Everybody including Carl checked on the first round. Then the dealer took three cards and placed them on the table. The ace of hearts, ace of spades and the seven of diamonds were placed on the table. The player sitting next to Carl on his right side was a young lady from Thailand who had beautiful green eyes.

Her hair was long and black. She was wearing a red dress and very attractive. She gave Carl a quick look to see if she could read his facial expressions. Carl looked back at her with a smile on his face.

"Oh yeah, I will have her sitting with me in the hot tub soon, located in my hotel suite". Carl said to himself as he knew what the outcome was going to be.

Carl was playing poker just for fun without any gain because he could create Zillions of dollars. He could have an unlimited amount of money at any given time. Most of all Carl did not use any of his power as he played poker with the other players. He didn't want to cheat at all. This was about pure skill and luck!

The next round of bets was placed before the fourth card came out on the table. The first person to place a bet was in the amount of $5,000. The green eyed Asian lady bet $8,000. Next Carl bet the same amount of $8,000 and waited for guy to his left to place a bet.

The man to Carl's left had a sour look on his face and folded his cards in for the dealer. The next player placed an $8,000 bet. Then the first player threw another $3,000 into the pot to make it an even $8,000.

The dealer brought out the fourth card and it was the jack of hearts. A lot of different looks were on everyone's faces when they all saw the fourth card come out. The first player checked. Next the green eyes lady bet $20,000 and then looked at Carl waiting for his response. Carl winked at her and placed the same $20,000 bet.

For some odd reason the player to Carl's left doubled the bet to $40,000. When this gentleman increased the bet it had no effect on the other players. Quickly without skipping a beat the rest of the players placed a total of $40,000 a piece into the pot.

The dealer puts out the fifth card and it's the ten of hearts. Carl knew he had this game won with the royal flush! However he showed no emotion to give away that he had this game in the bag. The first player bet $10,000. Without hesitation the beautiful lady next to Carl bets $100,000. The lady looked at Carl and said. "It's your turn handsome". Casually Carl bets $100,000 leans back in his chair and smiles at this beautiful Asian lady. The rest of the players folded their cards. Now it was Carl and the green eye goddess left.

    The lady checked and so did Carl right after. This fine lady looked at Carl and thought she had him beat. "I have four aces. Sorry but you lose sir"! She says as this sexy lady shows Carl the two aces in her hands. "That is a great hand you have there but I have something you need to see". Carl says as he puts a devilish grin on his face and reaches for his cards.

    The look on her face was classic after he showed her his cards. She went from pure confidence to I'm going to rip this motherfucker's throat out! "How did you do that"? The lady asked in shock and awe. "It was nothing but pure luck". Carl answered back. "As a matter of fact come with me and I will show you amazing things"! This beautiful looked at Carl and smiled. "What can you show me"? She asked Carl with curiosity in her smile.

    Carl took this ladies hand and within a blink of an eye both of them were inside the casino's best suite. Her mouth dropped as she couldn't believe what just happened. The suite was 10,000 square feet and with all of the luxury of a mansion.

    "How did you do that? How is this possible"? The lady asked. "Let's just say I'm a unique person that can make the impossible into a reality". After Carl said those words this sexy Asian lady took off her dress and let it fall to the floor. She wasn't wearing any bra or panties and looked perfect!

    Carl picked her up and carried her to the bed. As they made love there were two bottles of champagne sitting on the night stand. After an hour went by they took a break from fucking and opened both bottles to drink.

    "Who are you really"? The lady asked Carl as she sat comfortably in bed next to him. "Let's just say I'm a very lucky guy with a lot of power". Carl said with confidence and a devilish grin on his face.

"Then show me more of this power you possess". The lady said as her left hand was feeling all over Carl's body. "You will see". Carl said and immediately a whole new world opened inside the hotel suite.

Keep in mind Carl is still on a full blown acid trip seeing the same amount of intense visuals. Just like when he was on stage performing his magic in front on an audience.

Ten beautiful and perfect women were standing around the bed and each one of them held sliver plates. Each lady was wearing only body jewelry. But also every woman was a different ethnic race and wearing different body jewelry.

There were gifts on every plate. The bedroom and even the bed they were on was starting to expand. Two Siberian tigers were roaming around the room like Carl's personal guardians. Exotic birds were flying around and landing on the bed posts and chandlers.

Now the ten gifts each one of these amazingly beautiful women were holding was different then the next one. The first silver plate held five million dollars all in five hundred dollar bills stacked on top of each other.

The second plate held a mountain of cocaine. This pile of cocaine looked like a one hundred ounce pyramid of nose candy perfection!

On the third plate were twelve keys to twelve different sport cars. Each key belong to not just any sports car but only super or hyper sport cars. However with Carl's infinite power he can easily customize each vehicle the way he wants it.

There were jewels of all kinds in many shapes and colors on the fourth plate. These expensive stones were mesmerizing to look at and each one was from a different part of the world. The amount of money all of these jewels were worth at least a billion dollars if not more.

The fifth plate held a small six ounce bottle. The clear liquid inside this bottle was not LSD nor was it any other psychedelic drug. Inside this bottle contained the cure to every disease and sickness known to mankind!

All kinds of gourmet food was stacked a foot and a half high. Several fruits, meats, vegetables, cheeses, and bread were on top of the sixth plate.

Fifty little bottles of fine liquors were standing straight up on the seventh plate. Each one these bottles was ice cold to perfection and ready to drink.

There sitting on the eight plate was a device the size of a TV remote. This highly advanced technological device put outs a hologram with a simple touch of one button. This hologram held a new and unforeseen technology that was faster and far more advanced than any cell phone or super computer in the world!

On the ninth plate was a one liter bottle of pure drinking water. Water that was so pure when you drank just even a sip it would reverse the aging process. Meaning your physical body can go back ten years or even back to when you were twenty one years old.

On the tenth and last plate there sat a little monkey. A spider monkey in fact. Why this particular monkey you might be wondering. Because this monkey can speak all languages, can lift ten thousand times its own weight, will do anything you ask of and faster than any other animal in the world. So in other words this monkey is mankind's new best friend.

"What do you think of my power now"? Carl asked the green eyed lady as her eyes were wide open in complete amazement. "This is incredible". The young lady replied back. "How are you able to do this"? She asked with a surprised look on her face. "I can't tell you who, where or how I got this power. The only thing I can say it's a gift that was offered to me and I took it".

Both Carl and the Asian lady indulged themselves with the gifts on the plates. All of the ten ladies joined Carl and the Asian goddess on the bed. For the next eight hours Carl had himself a royal orgy that any man would dream of.

Towards the end of this unbelievable fantasy Carl was in a shower that was big enough for twenty people! Six of these perfect beautiful women were washing Carl from head to toe. These girls also brushed his teeth, cut his hair, clipped his nails and a shoulder massage. Most of all two of the girls were taking turns sucking his dick and gave him an intense release!

Meanwhile in the bedroom on the bed the green eyed Asian lady was getting her pussy licked by two ladies. The other two ladies were severing her high quality and expensive cocaine and liquor.

She was in pure heaven and loving every minute of it! But it's sad to say this girl's dream vacation was about to come to an end. Carl walked back into the bedroom with the six other women and they dressed him from head to toe.

"Are you having fun over there"? Carl asked the green eyed lady as she moaned in bed. "Well that definitely answers my question". Carl said he was fully dressed and petting one of the tigers.

"Ladies I'm sorry but I have to run. I have a lot to see and do". Carl said with a smile on his face. All of the ladies including the Asian with green eyes kissed Carl goodbye. One of them asked where he was going. Without saying a word Carl vanished in thin air. Once Carl left the ten ladies did too and the bedroom transformed back to its regular size.

The green eyed Asian lady was in complete shock as to what just happened! This beautiful young girl was unbelievably excited and grateful for the experience of a life time. Within seconds she repeatedly said. "Thank you Carl! Where ever you are thank you"! The young Asian lady walked out the hotel suite with a smile on her face and back into the casino.

Chapter 10

Carl traveled to the state of Maine by using teleportation. He wanted to visit a famous church he heard about. This church is located near the ocean with amazing views and beautiful architectural design! Saint Ann's church is the name and Carl was happy to visit it.

Near the edge of a cliff where the church would have their mass is where Carl appeared looking at the sunrise coming up and smiled. While smiling Carl thanked god in his own way for this powerful gift. He thanked god for the experience's he has had so far. Most of all Carl thanked god for choosing him to hold his awesome, amazing, infinite and incredible power!

After thirty minutes of watching the sunrise Carl walked inside the church to talk to god about other things. Once inside this beautiful and breath taking church Carl sat in the seventh row from the front.

"Jesus, god in heaven can you please forgive me for things I have done wrong in my life. I can never thank you enough for what you have given to me. I have accomplished so much by creating heaven on earth for all living things to live in happiness. But when this gift of mine is gone I want to rebuild what I have created. I need to find out how to do this while I still have time. The only way to accomplish this mission is to see everything in the future to come. That way I can remember what to do when this incredible power is gone."

Carl sat and continued to pray and talk to god in his own way. Fifteen minutes passed by. A man was walking up towards Carl casually. "Hello sir how is your day going"? This man asked Carl. "I'm doing great. Actually I'm living the dream of a lifetime! By the way I'm Carl. What is your name"? Carl said as he extended his hand. The man shook Carl's hand and said. "It's nice to meet you Carl my name is John".

As John shook Carl's hand something shocking happened! While shaking Carl's hand John knew exactly who Carl is! Instantly John knew

Carl was the one! The one who was chosen to hold the infinite power of god!

"You're him"! John said out loud. "I am him? Who am I"? Carl asked John. "You were chosen to hold the infinite power. The power of god! I know it because I once held its unbelievable power"!

"So you are thee John? The only one who has survived after your year was up". Carl asked as he stood in front of John with a shocking and yet feared look on his face.

Why would Carl fear this man when he cannot die? Plus Carl can do, become and have anything he wants. Why would he fear John? The real reason is because the mind John has is an evil one. Or can become consumed with evil and controlling intentions.

"Yes that's me. I am the only survivor. Tell me. How does it feel to hold the power of god"? John asked Carl with a grin on his face and a new look of curiosity in his eyes. "It's amazing and endless". Carl said but without any fear. Why no fear you might ask? Within seconds Carl would make this man disappear, like he never existed.

"Oh yes I know and I remember. I miss holding and having control of the power you have"! John said but now with an odd look on his face.

In the back of Carl's mind he could feel a tension that something was wrong. A feeling that possibly John was up to no good. Carl was careful as to what was going to happen next. Even though Carl could kill this man within a blink of an eye! Still he feared the mindset of John and at the same time had nothing to fear.

The smile almost goes away from john's face and then he asked. "Carl, can I ask you something? Can I ask you for a favor"? John said with his right out. He was hoping Carl would do him this favor. "What's the favor John"? Carl asked with caution in his voice. "Please give me just some of the power. All I need is a little bit of your almighty power that's it. Please give me some of your power I need to have it again"! John said intensely as he begged Carl with evil in his eyes. "John, please calm down and relax. I can't give you this power I'm sorry". Carl says. "But you can! I know that you can. Remember I once had the control and the power. I know the power you have and what you can do with it"! John said to Carl with greed in his teeth as he smiled like a sleazy demon. "You have the capability to share your infinite power with anyone". John explains.

Carl looked into this man's eyes and he knew not to listen to this evil and crazy fuck! What Carl saw into the eyes of John was fucking madness, greed, envy, self centered and unstoppable chaos! This was the opposite of who Carl is.

Even though John actually does have a good side to him as he works hard at the church. John never complains and is always grateful for what he has. He is also happy to live life every single day to help anyone he could.

However there is a sick, evil and dark side to John that he keeps locked away from the world he lives today. This is a side of John as you know is very destructive and sociopathic monstrous giant. Meaning he has no remorse for the horrible and unforgiveable things he has done in the past. However when John's time was done and he no longer contained this infinite power anymore, is when the fear took over! Most of all waking up in the woods naked, cold and then the repentance began.

"John, please relax and sit down with me". Carl said while holding his hands out. John sat down with Carl to talk. Carl tried his best to explain to John that he could not give any of his power to him. Even if Carl wanted to he knew for a fact this would be total insanity and the worse mistake he could make. John on the other hand was not listening to what Carl is explaining to him.

"Carl I know you mean well. But I don't need all of your power. Just a little bit of it. Please Carl I just need the power of money that's all. Nothing too big and nothing compared to the true power you hold"! John said with a huge grin on his face in hopes Carl will fold.

"John I'm sorry but I'm not going to do this for you. Joseph told me what you did when it was your time to hold this power". Carl said to John. But quickly that grin on John's face changed into an angry, evil and malevolent look of the devil himself.

"Now look here and listen to me good. I want that power of endless amounts of money and I want it now! Like I said you can give me this power. I know you are capable of sharing it because I once held its great power. You will give me this power now"! John yelled at Carl.

John was a man willing to do anything in order to make this world a better place. Only because of the horrific sins John committed when he once held the power. But the evil from within him couldn't be contained anymore. For John's gut instinct knew this was his last chance to have a little piece of god's power. And John wanted this power no fucking matter what!

Carl didn't say or do anything back to John. Carl was wise and powerful enough to know it was pointless. Besides Carl had better things to do with his time rather than sit around and argue with this asshole.

In milliseconds Carl once again vanished into thin air leaving behind John who was now even more pissed off that Carl had left the church. Although John was furious about Carl leaving without giving him the gift of money worldwide, John suddenly began praying because he wanted forgiveness for his wicked ways.

The evil within John fell back into the pit of his soul as the good came back and continued growing again in him. Because the evil of human beings will always be there even after heaven on earth was created. The positive and light will always keep the darkness at bay. It will never go away.

Chapter 11

The next stop Carl is going to make is appearing on top of the Himalayan Mountains. Instant teleportation is of course what Carl used to get there. Carl lets out a sigh of relief as he could see his breath because of how cold it was.

"Thank god I'm away from that crazy asshole". Carl said out loud as he looked around seeing the awesome scenery. Carl took a few minutes to calm himself down. He wanted to focus on what needed to be accomplished.

Carl wanted know how to see everything in the vast future to come. This intelligent and quick witted man knew this in his heart and inside his own mind, but for some reason he could not figure it out. Even with all of the power in the universe Carl could not find the answers he was searching for.

This drove him bat shit fucking crazy as he screamed out into the wind. "Fuck, why can't I figure this out"! Angry at himself Carl still tried to focus on what he needed in order to achieve this new level of knowledge and power!

Then it came to him unbelievably fast like getting struck by lightning but without warning. "She has the answers. The goddess known as mother can tell me. I remember what she said". Carl said with a smile on his face with a boost of confidence.

"I am the lizard king I know everything. This is what the goddess said to me". Carl said as he laughed.

Carl knew what needed to be done. He of course now has the power but needed the knowledge and wisdom the goddess has in order to complete his goal. With a smile on Carl's face and new look of hope Carl once again was ready to launch into the infinite universes and realms of existence.

A customized lazy boy recliner formed behind Carl as he quickly falls back into the chair. Four beautiful women appeared and each one of them was wearing nothing but a thong and exotic psychedelic tattoos. But good news the cold had no effect on them because Carl designed them this way.

In front of Carl stood a five foot hookah with now a thousand grams of 100% pure DMT! One the girls started giving Carl a shoulder massage, another was massaging his feet while one lady handed Carl a long hose attached to the hookah.

A blue flame appeared in the fourth girls hand to light the DMT as Carl leaned back in the recliner. Mr. Smith inhaled half of the DMT which is a lot of smoke! This was more than enough to fully blast off into the great beyond! However with Carl's power he was able to hold back from fully launching but the visuals were coming in extremely strong!

"It is time". Carl said after he exhaled the smoke. Now Carl takes the final drag filling up his lungs and most of his body! He held in the smoke for twenty seconds and then closed his eyes as exhaled the smoke.

    Here we go again people hang on tight! Boom! Carl finally launches into hyper drive and traveling at speeds so fast he even went beyond ludicrous speed. Billions of factual designs passed by Carl as he cried out to mother.

    "Goddess I'm back. I need your help. Please I need your knowledge"! Carl yelled out as his voice echoed through the wormholes of infinite existence. There were endless patterns constantly changing all around him. There were millions of eyes following and watching Carl as he traveled through these worm holes. A better way to describe what Carl was flying through is like a psychedelic time warp that looked never ending.

    Seconds later the portal stopped and Carl entered a world filled with skyscrapers that continuously moved and transformed into beings, other buildings, animals and multiple beams of light! Visually this was absolutely hypnotizing to watch and witness.

Now that Carl was use to this form of conciseness and level of existence confidently he hovered high in the air observing everything below. "Mother I need your help. I need your help goddess". Carl cried out after he looked around for thirty seconds. Again Carl cried out to the goddess known as mother but she did not appear. There was no answer from her either.

Without warning a loud sound came from below, Carl looked down to see what was causing this sound. A massive crack in the ground formed and spread causing the buildings to separate. Then a deep hole opened up but this hole was moving. The hole was breathing and constantly moving like a giant organism.

Carl was curious to see what was causing this hole to form and move. Buildings were still moving and expanding but other beings were shocked at what they were seeing. The looks on these beings faces were horrified as they the hole was becoming bigger like a giant mouth. This mouth was not only moving around and breathing but swallowing whatever came near it.

Carl watched this hole become more massive and could see the fear on the beings faces. Down this vast hole was absolute darkness. A darkness that looked endless.

Carl put his left hand out and used the power of god to stop this hole from swallowing this spiritual world into nothing. Even with Carl's awesome power he could not stop this ultimate juggernaut from feeding and eating this world alive!

"Fuck why can't I stop this thing". Carl screamed at the top of his lungs as he now used both of his hands to try to kill this monster from hell. Carl honestly was trying his best to stop this living apocalypse and the havoc it was causing but something was overriding his power.

"I hold the power of god! How can I not stop this thing"? Carl cried out as he kept trying his best to destroy this world eating monster. No matter what Carl tried this evil bastard was becoming bigger, stronger and little by little was swallowing the world Carl was standing on.

From within the depths of this enormous demon emerged a blue light that quickly came up the hole. The light fired out of this great hole like a blast from laser cannon! The good news is this blast did not destroy anything. The bad news is this blast of blue light took a hold of Carl completely.

This blue light formed into two hands each with ten fingers on each one. Quickly these hands of blue light pulled Carl down into the hole with blinding speeds.

"Fuck"! Carl yelled out as he was forced into a downward spiral of this blue light. Carl was going through twists and turns that he had no control of. He tried to stop himself from traveling further into this vortex by stretching out his arms and holding onto the walls. Within a split second the pull from this awesome force broke both of Carl's arms shattering his bones from within side.

The good news is Carl was in his spiritual form and not his physical. Without feeling any pain Carl repaired his arms in half of a second and stretched his arms forward as he continued to travel through this monster vortex. Still maneuvering through the unpredictable twists and turns Carl stopped himself by using his tremendous power and force.

For only five seconds Carl was able to stop in the middle of this vortex. Then the blue light grabbed a hold of Carl once again and pulled him faster through the vortex than before!

Carl screamed as loud as he could, trying to stop himself by unleashing his full power. But nothing worked! Something was definitely overriding Carl's power or at least counter acting it.

Finally the vortex pushed and spit out Carl onto a lake. Quickly Carl landed his feet on the water and he glided across the water like he was water skiing.

Carl entered into another world surrounded by mountains with hundreds of waterfalls and forests. This perfect landscape was a form of heaven filled with positive energy. Carl was still gliding through the lake and then slowed down until he came to a complete stop standing on top of the water.

For only a few seconds Carl looked around at this new and mind blowing world he was in. A lady slowly came up from the water head first within twenty feet from Carl. Her hair and eyes were both bright red as she risen up from the lake. Her body was built to perfection as she was now fully out of the water and walking towards Carl.

"So you want to talk to our goddess. Why do you want to speak to our mother"? This beautiful redhead lady of perfection asked Carl as she was walking closer to him. "I need the goddess's help. I'm looking for answers that she might know". Carl said calmly as this beautiful lady walked toward him with a smile on her face.

"I know what you want and I know what you need". The lady said with a smile on her face as she put her hand on Carl's forehead. She did this to read his mind and look into Carl's third eye. Yes believe it or not your third eye does exist in the spiritual world along with the rest of you.

"What is it that I need"? Carl asked this lady as she slowly takes her hand off his forehead with a smile on her face. The lady did not saying but the smile on her face grew even bigger. Twenty naked perfect women appeared around Carl and each one was different than the other.

"This is what I need"? Carl asked as he looked at all of the women around him. "It's what you need and what you want". The lady with the red hair and eyes said as the other ladies tried to seduce Carl. Two girls were sucking his dick while the rest of them were licking his spiritual body from head to toe.

"This is not why I am here. Where is mother? Where is the goddess? I need her help now"! Carl yelled out and then the girls stopped. All of them were straight up and looked at Carl with disappointing written all over their faces.

One second later all twenty women fused into the red haired lady as one spiritual being. This perfect red eye lady started laughing out loud as her whole body shook with vibrations from her laughter. This woman's laughter caused her body to then spontaneously combust into a hundred different birds not from our world.

Each bird was colorful in a beautiful design and amazing to look at. However each one of these birds does not exist in the physical world on planet earth. So Carl witnessed and experienced something he never seen before.

These birds flew over Carl's head and into the mountains. Not to worry, none of these birds took a shit on Carl's head as they flew over him. However Carl did watch a hundred different colorful trails these birds left behind. He watched the birds fly into the mountains behind him.

From out of nowhere a voice cried out like a sonic boom and said. "Well hello handsome. I heard you needed my help and I'm happy you came back to me". This voice came from the goddess known as mother. Although Carl could not see her at first but she was all around him.

"Goddess, yes I do need your help. I know you have the answers that I need". Carl said as he kept looking around to see where she was. There was no reply but only silence as Carl waited for the goddess to say anything to help him.

"Mother I'm begging you please! I need your help now"! Carl screamed out into the open air as he was now on his knees in the water. A few seconds after Carl cried out to the goddess he felt an enormous earthquake erupting. Even though Carl was still on the water he could still feel this tremendous force all around him. That's how powerful this earthquake was becoming and it grew stronger by the milliseconds.

The whole world was moving and shifting all around Carl. The lake, trees, animals, mountains and even the sky was transforming. Carl flew a couple of feet up from the water watching everything collapsing and transform into something.

Less than a minute flew by quick as a vast darkness surrounded Carl from behind him. Right in front of Carl was once the world he was in and now the world became the size of a basket ball.

"What the fuck is going on here"? Carl said as the small world was imploding into nothing. Just before the world disappeared it became the size of a grain of sand from the Mojave Desert.

Boom! A loud burst of sound and golden energy shot out from this ball of golden energy. This almighty sound echoed through the vast darkness as Carl could feel the warmth from the energy in front of him. Beams of light emerged from this baseball size of pure energy.

"Goddess is that you"? Carl asked this golden sphere in front of him and Carl was right! This source of energy is mother who is now quickly growing stronger. Another loud burst of energy echoed through the darkness once again. However this time the goddess fully appeared in her spiritual body yelling out loud with her awesome power! Only this time she stood one hundred feet tall.

The awesome sight of this goddess is still mind blowing! Again mother has long golden hair flowing everywhere, a perfect physical body and an endless amount of power and energy. This energy emerged from within her creating this unlimited power! This time mother took the form of another perfect female.

"Welcome back Carl. I heard you missed me and need my help"! The goddess said and then snapped her fingers. A new world spit out into existence after the loud crack from snapping her fingers. This world was a small single island with waves constantly crashing onto the beach.

There at last was mother who stood one hundred feet high hovering a foot off the ground in front of Carl. "Mother I do need your help and thank you for coming". Carl said as he held his hands together praying to her. "Carl I have always been here. When you enter this realm of this existence, I was always here". The goddess explained to Carl as she looked down on him.

"You were there when that hole opened and swallowed me? The lady with red hair and eyes along with her twenty perfect servants, you were there? But how I never saw you there"? Carl asked the goddess with his arms open because he was confused.

"Carl I am all of those things you experience and more. Why are you praying to me when you are a god"? Mother asked with a slight disappointment in her voice.

"I'm praying to you because I need your help mother." Carl said to her in hope she can help him. "You want to see into the future and obtain this knowledge in your memory so you can help your world after the year is up and the power is gone". Mother says to Carl with a smile on her face. 'Yes, but how do you know this"? Carl asked the goddess with confusion in his voice.

Mother looked down at Carl as she walked around him with still a smile on her face. However she was becoming annoyed with Carl.

"You once said I am the lizard king, I can do anything. That is why when you first met me I said to you. I am the lizard king, I know everything". Mother explained to Carl and then stopped walking to look down at him.

The goddess then kneeled down to look at Carl closer. Mother then said this to Carl. "You are a god! You have god's unlimited power"! The goddess yelled at Carl. "Your right and I do have the power! But I don't know how to use this part of my power". Carl says to mother pledging with her to show him how to use this power and find the answers he seeks.

"You are a god"! The goddess cries out spewing forth her awesome power and golden energy everywhere. "I do not tolerate weakness from a mortal or anyone"! This goddess screams at Carl with furious anger. Mother is now really fucking pissed off and puts Carl through her ultimate test!

The goddess stands up and kicked Carl like a football through the goal posts. Carl then stopped himself in mid air after he flew backwards three hundred yards.

"Unleash your true power. Show me what you really got. You want to know about the future then give me everything you got"! Mother yelled at Carl with tremendous anger and a sonic blast in her voice! The goddess was still standing a hundred feet tall awaiting Carl's response with a horrifying and angry look on her face. "Now show me your power"! Mother screams louder than ever before at Carl displaying and unleashing her golden power all around her.

It only took Carl two seconds to think of his next move of attack. Behind Carl a massive thunder and lightning storm appeared from his own thoughts. Boom! Carl launched like a cannon firing straight towards mother. Just before he reached mother Carl transformed himself into a two hundred foot Tyrannosaurs Rex and landed right on top of her.

    With no hesitation the T-Rex takes one giant bite and rips off the goddess's head and swallows it whole. The T-Rex then raises his head into the air and lets out an earth shattering roar with strikes of white lightning hitting the water behind this great beast. Meanwhile this mean looking storm in the background was gaining strength and moving over Carl and mother's headless body.

    Before the T-Rex could take another bite the goddess's right arm quickly extended and reached out grabbing the throat of the T-Rex. Right after her hand squeezes with an iron grip a blast of golden light and energy fires out of the mouth from the T-Rex.

    The light turns into a circular blade that is spinning at a high speed. A split second later the golden blade flies straight through the T-Rex's neck cutting off the head. But before the head falls to the ground, Carl lunges forward in his human form and catches his head. Carl puts his head back on top of his shoulders before touching the ground.

The goddess's body leaps into the air with her head reappearing on her body. Then the circular blade reattaches to her body and now she is ready to take Carl to school and destroy this man!

Nevertheless neither one of the ultimate beings can die. So in reality it's a catch twenty two. However the goddess was doing this intentionally so Carl can become more human than human. And use his full potential with the infinite power he holds.

"Good try and nice attack. Get ready Carl"! The goddess yells as she raises he arms in the air. Billions or even trillions of sharp golden objects appear and were aimed at Carl.

He gets himself ready before she throws these blades at him. Carl jumps into the air at her but before he can dodge any of the blades. A thousand of these blades hit him at blinding speed.

Before Carl notices that mother is not in front of him anymore she is right behind him and grabs Carl by his nut sack throwing him into the ocean. Slowly coming out of the water is Carl's left middle finger screaming fuck you to the goddess.

Mother now has a smile on her face but is still pissed off with furious anger and ready to show Carl all of her tricks. Carl's middle finger is still up and now taunting her as he curls his middle finger repeatedly.

"You weak mortal, you taunt me with your pathetic finger"! The goddess yells at Carl as she flies into the ocean to show him who the real god is. Once mother entered into the water ten feet deep Carl was already out of the ocean and hovering in the air looking down at the waves.

With a quick blink of his eyes, Carl froze the entire ocean along with the goddess in it. At the same time Carl is smoking a two foot blunt and says this. "Come on mother; show me what you got beautiful". Carl exhales a thick cloud of white smoke with a smile on his face as he awaits her next move.

Multiple loud cracks of thunder explode at the same time all around Carl. These extremely loud bursts of sound scared the living shit out of Carl as he could feel the electricity in his teeth from the lightning.

Fifty bolts of white lightning strike Carl and hold onto him keeping him suspended in the air. Two seconds later the frozen ocean transformed into a yeti standing over a thousand feet tall at it smiles and watches Carl. Even though Carl can turn off the pain the lightning keeps Carl suspended in the air. While the lightning ran through his body Carl kept pretending he was in pain by screaming loud!

As the yeti keeps smiling as he watches but Carl stops screaming and now is smiling straight at this great white giant. Carl then turns into thousands of killer bees and escapes the lightning by flying into the nose of this monstrous yeti. As these killer bees sting and bite the yeti from with inside this great monster, the yeti screams and roars in constant pain.

The yeti continues to scream in pain and agony. But not for long as it all comes to an end as the head of this yeti explodes and there is Carl hovering in the air. He is covered in flames like the human torch as the body of the yeti falls into the ocean.

After Carl watches the yeti's corpse sink into the depths of the ocean he looks to his left down to the beach. On the beach is the goddess laying in a long beach chair getting her finger and toe nails done by several different women.

"Are you having fun playing with your toys Carl"? The goddess says to him with a smile on her face as she looks at Carl with glowing golden eyes. Now Carl was becoming angry as she mocked him. The new human torch has now grown to a hundred feet tall screamed in a pure fit of rage! Huge flames not only became his body but were spitting outward.

The goddess held up her right hand and waved it towards Carl with a twist of her wrist. Carl at full throttle flies straight towards mother screaming "You won't stop me"! Once again mother waves her right hand and hundreds of mini me versions her appear. Each one of them was four feet tall and with a different weapon in their hands.

All of the mini goddess's attacked Carl at the same time. Some of them burned before getting a direct hit on Carl. But there was too many to handle so Carl starts multiplying into fifty versions of the human torch. Even with Carl's quick thinking and clever counter attacks mother was always ten steps ahead of him.

Meanwhile the goddess is still on the beach relaxing, eating grapes, getting a foot massage and smoking hash out of a hookah. All as she watches Carl having fun with now thousands of herself.

Oh yeah mother is one crafty bitch! She smiles watching this battle rage on. But then a feeling comes over her. Mother looks to her left and sees Carl sitting in a lawn chair smoking her hash.

"Hi handsome, it looks like you're getting the hang of this". The goddess says with her eyes wide open. Carl is in his regular form relaxing and responds by saying "Remember I am the lizard king I can do anything". "This is true Carl but can you do this"? Mother says as she creates a copy or a clone of Carl. This new clone is right between her legs licking her pussy like it's the last free meal. Carl is stunned to see she can make a clone from him that quick.

"If you think that's impressive Carl I can also make you kill yourself". The goddess yells out as she holds Carl's head that's between her legs having the time of his life.

Right in front of Carl appeared three clones of him and two of them had giant custom knifes. The two clones with knifes grabbed the third clone and viciously stabbed him repeatedly. The third clone was screaming from the intense pain and covered in blood from head to toe within less than a minute.

Quickly Carl snaps his fingers and makes all four of the clones disappear. "Oh come on, what's the matter Carl? Don't you love my sense of humor"? Mother laughs as her voice echoes everywhere. "Cute joke goddess, but look at the battle going on up there". Carl says as he points his finger to the sky. "Yes your right Carl it looks like a lot of fun up there". The goddess of perfection says. "Let's go join them". Carl says and instantly both of them join the fight as the war rages from up above.

Fifty human torches fought and battled thousands of little goddess. All of them were stabbing, hitting, shooting, decapitating, burning and many other vicious acts of violence to each other. This was an awe struck sight of a bloody and painful war of madness!

A split second later mother the great goddess pulls herself together, all five thousand versions of her back into one. It was an awesome sight seeing the goddess hovering in front of all fifty clones of Carl. The goddess waits as she smiles at all of them. Meanwhile the fifty clones of Carl were all in gulfed with red and orange flames. He was definitely ready for her next move.

"Are you having fun yet Carl? Or am I to much for you"? Carl responded by fusing back into one being. But this time Carl was his usual self and not the human torch. "How can I see into the future? Please tell me how it works. Why won't you just tell me"? Carl yells in a fit of confusion and anger.

The goddess with a look of disappointment shakes her head as the rain falls on them both. "You fucking idiot! You have learned so much and at the same time you have learned nothing"! Mother yells at Carl as her face shifts and changes with frustration.

"Mother what is it that I need to learn? I have been trying to figure it out! That's why I'm here. I need your wisdom and your help". Carl says with his arms open and a look of desperation painted all over his face. But before the goddess responded to Carl she disappears into nothing. Then Carl looks around to see where she ran off to. "Ok. Where the hell did she go this time and what the fuck is she up to now"? Carl says to himself.

Out of nowhere a great voice spoke to Carl. The voice surrounded Carl from all angles as he kept looking to see where the voice was coming from this time.

"You still have to prove to me that you are worthy to obtain this advanced knowledge. Now show and prove to me your true power"! The goddess yelled as her words sound more like pure thunder colliding together. "I'm ready mother! Now show yourself to me"! Carl screams as his energy level rises higher than ever before.

Carl's screams turns into a roar of a real god! His body becomes a bright neon blue light almost identical to mother's golden light. His power and energy level increases rapidly. Carl is now becoming what the goddess has been looking for and what she has been waiting for too.

"That's it, come on show me more"! The voice of this incredible goddess yells and cries out. "Then show yourself to me! Where are you"? Carl screams out in a fit of rage and madness. "I'm right here rookie"! The great goddess of Mother Nature screams at Carl only a few inches away from his face.

Now the real war begins! The ultimate battle against these two gods has begun! You will witness and see the god's unleashing their true power! This is Carl's greatest test of all time.

Quickly Carl flies backwards within a split second leaving behind four clones of him to attack her. But before Carl could watch his clones rip mother apart she appears in front of him. The goddess grabs Carl quicker than you can blink. She kisses him shoving her tongue down his throat without hesitation.

"Nice move but you can show me better than that"! Mother says to Carl and then she rips his throat out turning him into a human pez dispenser. No blood came gushing out of Carl's neck instead the blue energy closed his throat insanely fast!

"You got it bitch? Here it comes"! Carl screams and then creates a trap for her. Carl throws a blue ball of light at the goddess. This blue light turns into device that will contain this wild and unstoppable goddess.

It worked! Carl's energy trapped the goddess in the air and she could not move. However this clever maneuver made mother angrier than ever before. Mother's voice echoes and screams out even though her lips don't move.

"You fool. I said to show me better. Now unleash and show me your ultimate power"! The goddess screams as she breaks through Carl's weak containment displaying her furious power and energy. Quickly her golden energy expands fast and starts forming into an actual sun that blinds Carl.

More and more power the goddess unleashes with a mega sound louder than ever! Mother becomes this sun as it keeps expanding and blinding Carl so he cannot see anything. However seconds later Carl's eyes changes and adapts to the light so he can see.

Carl takes one huge breath and starts inhaling the sun's energy. At the same instant Carl's spiritual body increasingly becomes bigger! Now he has a mixture of both blue and golden energy flowing through him.

One hundred feet in front of Carl was the goddess now smiling as she now approves Carl's decision and quick wit. "That's it handsome. Now show mother what you can really do". The goddess yells as her voice becomes louder.

"Fuck you"! Carl screams in an uncontrollable madness as he now fires an atomic blast of energy at the goddess. This atomic blast looks more like an energy attack coming from a fusion version of Vegeta and Goku. These characters are of course from dragon ball z and super.

This enormous blast of power hits the goddess perfectly. When the smoke clears there she is still hovering in mid air crossing her arms without any damage. Mother lets out a quick laugh and then cries out "Show me your power"! And oh fuck now its coming. Mother fires back but with now half of the world behind her fusing into one energetic massive attack.

    Carl uses his quick wit and sticks out his right hand to not stop but slow down her attack on him. Meanwhile Carl's left hand is aimed at the water below. He brings up the ocean at first and then the thunder storm from above to collide into one ultimate natural force!

    While Carl slows down mother's attack to give him enough time to fire back. His attack with the ocean and the storm turning into billions of heavy metals so massive she can't see anything. Then it dawns on Carl as his attack hits mother. "I got it"! Carl says as he now figures out what the goddess has been saying all along. Show me your fucking power!

With a quick and simple snap of his fingers Carl turns the world they both were in and changes it into another completely different planet. A world filled with volcanoes, rivers of lava, forests fires, mountains spewing blood and lava as the sky is filled with explosions of fire. A planet made of nightmarish, unpredictable chaos, and devastating extreme horrors! Some people might say you could call this place hell.

Six clones of mother surround Carl and they all say this at the same time "Now you're getting warmer you fucking mortal"! The goddess then flies backwards screaming "Unleash your power"! With pure rage and furious anger the goddess spits out her golden energy while she screams letting out a sonic boom from her mouth.

However Carl disappears just before her sonic boom reaches him. Although mother cannot see Carl she can still feel his presence all around her. Slowly the goddess grows a positive grin on her face as she closes her eyes.

"Good now show me what you got"! The goddess says out loud because she knows where Carl is. He hasn't left this planet because Carl became the planet in which he has created. More and more volcanoes are made within seconds while the explosions in the sky were getting closer to the goddess.

"That's it rookie. Bring it"! The goddess cries out as she prepares herself for the wrath of Carl's power. Over twenty volcanoes erupted and launched out of their hellish mouths tons of lava hotter than hell itself towards her. From up above the explosions of fire gathered into one horrific monstrous figure with the face of a fiery demon. Once the face of this nightmare finally formed a smiled at mother as she smiled back awaiting its next move.

"I am a little impressed. Do it, do it now"! The goddess yells with a smile on her face and her eyes are wide open. From up above and way down below both forces fired their fury at mother. She was now engulfed in fire, lava and explosions all at once! The goddess did not move an inch as she took on this astronomic attack from Carl.

The goddess cannot feel any pain nor will her spiritual body take on any damage. She laughs as the attacks hit her and they just keep coming. However there was more to come.

The world was now moving, shifting and closing in on the goddess. Quickly the entire planet started to slip in half and then folded to crush this goddess. But like she said before "You are powerful Carl but you will never be as powerful as me"!

Once the planet fully enclosed on the goddess the world looked like a giant flat piece of fire and brimstone! "Can you feel it, can you see it Carl. I know how close you are. Tell me can you see it"? The goddess asks Carl as she is stuck with inside this containment of fire and explosive chaos.

But Carl doesn't respond right away and at the same time the goddess can feel him. She can feel every emotion and thought from Carl. This is not because the two gods are fused together but for the fact she has the power and ability to do so.

"Tell me what you see Carl. Your there, I know that you are". Mother says still strapped inside this planet of hell fire. But without warning or Carl saying anything the unthinkable and the incredible is now happening.

The flat planet that was once a nightmare of torturous burning, suffering, pain and agony has now transformed. Carl not only turned this new world into something better with beautiful landscapes but into the future that would eventually become reality on earth.

"What did you see, what are you seeing now"? Mother asks in a relaxing tone of voice as she swims backwards in a crystal clear river of perfection. This new world of earth was amazing and awe inspiring. This was the future that could be because Carl created it to be.

Now honestly and truthfully way before this world was created inside Carl's spiritual mind and body he had already traveled millions of years into the future of not only planet earth itself but all of existence. However all Carl needed to do was become and travel twenty years into the future in order to change it for the greater good and to change the future for everyone to benefit from.

    Carl finally found the answers he was looking for and a new hope that was once fucking impossible has now become a positive reality for all living and non living things. Don't worry I will explain what new knowledge and experiences Carl has gathered soon. And yes this is Mark Talese talking to you. I have been talking to you this entire time!

    "Come here and relax with me Carl". The goddess asked as she now was hanging out in a hot tub filled with purified mineral water. Carefully and slowly Carl walks towards mother as he transitions from being the planet back to his spiritual form.

    "Now you know how to use your power completely we don't have to battle anymore". The goddess said as Carl walks into the hot tub to join her. "I like you Carl even though I was frustrated at times. But I still like you. I have always liked you. Mother said as she relaxed in the water with a beautiful smile on her face.

"Mother how did you or do you know all of this? But why didn't you just tell me instead of us beating the shit out of each other"? Carl asked as he had a look of confusion on his face. "The reason why is because I needed you to work for it and find the answers yourself. Even if meant both us going to war with each other. I already knew this was the answer and the only possible way to find what you were looking for. Remember Carl I am the lizard king. I know everything"!

With a new feeling and understanding Carl had another level of respect for mother the goddess of endless existence, universes and time. The goddess of Mother Nature! Once again mother could feel and know every thought and emotion from Carl.

"I know you have a good heart Carl and a good sense of direction. Even though I know how much of a perverted fuck you are". Mother says as Carl smiles back at her. "That's why I'm going to give this gift. This gift will help you in many endless ways". The goddess says to him and then she stands up inside the hot tub and walks over to him.

    Knowledge can be the greatest gift of all time. However at the same time it can be extremely dangerous. Always try to use whatever power you hold for positive things.

    The goddess kisses Carl as she fuses her spiritual body into his becoming one ultimate and unique mega powerful spiritual being. Both energies combine into one awesome force unleashing outwards and spreading beyond the world they were both in. Their combined power spreads throughout the vast multiple universes but in a positive and peaceful way.

    The goddess gave Carl her greatest power of all. The power of endless knowledge! Not only was Carl able to see and become the future he also has achieved her endless power of knowledge and all the answers to every question. The knowledge of the past, present and what is to come.

    Mother then breaks from Carl's spiritual body and back into her own. Causally she sits back down to relax again. "Out of the one hundred and one mortal human beings who possessed the power of the infinite card, the power of god, you are the only mortal I have met. This is something truly special and amazing because you are the one. The one that Joseph and the universe have been looking for. You are the chosen one who can change the world for the greater". Mother says to Carl.

    "Thank you goddess, thank you for everything but at the same time I can never thank you enough for what you have given to me". Carl said as nothing but positive energy emerged from him and surrounded him. "Do what needs to be done Carl. This is how you can thank me, Joseph, the gods and the universes". The goddess says with a good meaningful laugh. "You have to go for now because your trip is now ending". Mother says.

"Wait. You said the gods. You mean there are several gods"? Carl asks in a mind now full of confusion. Then the next thought came to him from this new and infinite knowledge. Carl realizes there are several gods and many other things he did not know about. So Carl smiles and takes in this new wisdom.

"Bye handsome, I'll see around Carl". The goddess says as she becomes smaller because Carl now flies backwards into a worm hole.

Carl travels through this psychedelic portal back to the physical world and into his body that was laying back in the lazy boy recliner. It take mush time as Carl's spiritual body hits his physical body so hard it knocks him out of the chair and off the Himalaya Mountains! As Carl is free falling downward he could see the little faces of the beautiful women who were there to comfort his physical body while he was gone.

The ladies were watching him fall as they wave him goodbye but Carl puts a smile on his face and then turns around to face the valley below.

Quickly he picks up speed and flies straight into the ground and through the earth's core and out the other side of the planet. This only took Carl a few seconds to reach the other side of the earth.

After Carl ends up on other side of the earth he sits down on a boulder next to a river. Carl lifts his head up to the sky and sighs while a smile forms on his face. As the sun shines on his face Carl could feel both pure happiness and joy because he had completed his mission.

"I finally did it! But mother I thank you for giving me your power. Dam this is incredible knowing everything about the future. Even with my eyes closed I can see every event that will take place". Carl says and then stands up.

Further down the river Joseph appeared and was keeping an eye on Carl just to see what he's up to. Although Joseph was only there observing and watching Carl he wondered about what his next move is.

Joseph smiles at Carl with a drink in his hand. I believe he was drinking crown royal on ice this time. However Joseph smiled because he knew Carl had achieved two things. The first was become the future and knowing everything about it. The second was having mother's power of infinite knowledge. For this was truly something special. Carl will accomplish goals and many great things in the near future to come.

    This is why Joseph holds a smile on his face, because he always knew Carl was the one. He is the only one out of many people who was not consumed and selfish greed while having the power of god.

    After Carl lights a blunt the size of a Cuban cigar as he stands up from the boulder and takes off to see the world. Once again Carl travels in style as he flies through the clear skies in a customized craft of his own design. Without any noise the craft takes off beyond the speed of sound.

    "Good job kid, I am proud of you. And god speed". Joseph says as he raises his glass in the air. It looked as almost he was toasting to Carl. Joseph vanishes into nothing but he does it in style as he takes the last sip of his drink just before he is fully gone.

Chapter 12

"Thank you ladies and here's a tip for you". Carl says as he tips the girls millions of dollars. "Is there anything we can do for you Carl"? One of the girls asked him as he walks out of the hot tub. This tub was big enough to fit twelve people or more.

"Actually yes, if somebody can help dry me off I would greatly appreciate it". Carl asks and four ladies quickly walk over with towels in their hands. "Thank you girls, you are all doing an excellent job. How much longer until we arrive in Toronto Canada"? Carl asked his pilot.

"We should be arriving in less than three hours. If you don't mind me asking sir but why are we going to Toronto"? The pilot of the craft asked. "I'm going to visit an old friend of mine. Now let's speed things up a little bit". Carl says as they all can feel the craft picking up tremendous speed. Within fifteen minutes Carl and his crew finally reach Toronto Canada.

Carl's old friend Allen was getting off work and heading home. Allen stopped in a local bar for a few drinks to help take away the stress from the day. Allen orders himself a pint of moose head beer after he sits down at the bar. Ten minutes later as Allen was drinking his beer Carl casually walks through the door. Carl knew exactly where Allen would be because of the new power he now possess.

Carl carefully walks behind Allen and quickly up to him. "How have you been old friend"? Carl says to Allen as he stands on Allen's left hand side and leaning on the bar. Allen looks at his old high school friend Carl in complete shock and awe!

"Carl, how the fuck did you get here and when did you get here? Jesus it's good to see you man. "When the hell did you get here"? Allen asked Carl as he shook his hand. "Well I was in the area and I saw you walk into this bar. So I walked in to see how you were doing and it's been a long time since I saw you at our high school graduation"! Carl explains to Allen with a smile on his face.

"Fuck man it has been that long! Well here sit down and I'll buy you a drink"! Allen says to Carl as he is still excited to see him. "Allen, don't worry it, watch". Carl says and then snaps his fingers and pints of moose head lager appear on the bar. "Holy fuck, what are you a magician now? Carl how did you do that"? Allen asked as he was amazed at Carl's new capabilities. Allen touched the pint of beer just to see if it was even real but when he did Allen was more surprised that the beer was real.

"Allen you have no idea of what I can do now. Go ahead and take a sip. Let me know how it is". Carl says as he folds his arms together waiting for Allen to try his beer. Allen takes a sip then stops to look at the glass then proceeds to drink more with amazement. Allen was amazed at how perfect and cold the beer was.

"Dam Carl it tastes better than the first beer I had. How did you do this? What's your secret"? Allen asked as he held his pint glass in the air. Carl took a sip of his beer and answered Allen's question. "A while back I ran into a fortune teller who gave me this power. I didn't think it was possible at first until I realized and found out myself this power is very real"!

"No shit, well can you show me what else this power of yours can do"? Allen asked Carl and then started drinking the rest of his beer. Carl had a grin on his face and said to Allen "Stand up and check this out". So Allen stood up from the bar stool still holding his beer. "Ok, now what"? Allen asked as he waited for Carl to make something happen. Without snapping his fingers this time

Carl transformed the bar into a labyrinth palace filled with top models from around the world.

There were pools, hot tubs, fountains, bars, luxury furniture, buffets customize for a king and much more! Allen was paralyzed from the state of shock he was in. But who wouldn't be after going from being in a bar to this amazing palace that most people would only dream of.

"Allen, look at what you did. You're fucking pissing yourself"! Carl said as Allen continued pissing his pants. "Carl where are we and what is this place"? Allen asked as he finally unfroze himself and stopped pissing himself. "I'll explain after we get you cleaned up". Carl said. "We, what do you mean by that"? Allen asked and then six beautiful and perfect ladies escorted Allen to a customized bath tub.

All six girls took off Allen's clothes quickly. These ladies then walked with him into this luxurious bath tub to thoroughly clean Allen. Meanwhile Carl waited at the bar kicking back and relaxing as he let Allen enjoy himself.

After an hour and a half went by Allen was out of the tub, dried off and wearing new clean clothes that these ladies put on him. Quickly Allen walked over to Carl who was hanging out at the bar drinking ice cold patron straight out of the bottle. Carl smiles as he holds out his right hand to shake Allen's hand.

"Ok now tell me how you can make all of this happen"? Allen says as he shakes Carl's hand with a look of amazement in his eyes. "Allen the only way I can explain it in a way that makes sense, is I now hold the power of god"! Carl said. "You hold the power of god, so you are god now? If this true then bring my mother back to life". Allen asked Carl.

"I remember your mom Allen. I was there at her funeral back when we were fifteen years old. I'm sorry man but I can't bring your mom back from the dead". Carl explained to Allen. "But you are god and you hold god's power. Why can't you bring my mother back from the dead"? Allen asked. "Because this was part of the deal I made and it's one out of the six rules I cannot break. I have this power for exactly one year. With this power there are six rules that I cannot break even if I try to break them".

"One of these rules is you cannot bring back anything to life before you are given this power. But for example if a hundred people died yesterday then yes I can bring them all back to life". Carl says to Allen.

"How long have you had this power for"? Allen asked Carl "I've had this power for only a few months. So I have nine more months left until this power is gone and the gift is over with". Carl says. "But Allen I'm sorry that I can't bring your mom back. I remember how much you missed her after her funeral".

Allen had a disappointed look on his face because he had high hopes Carl could bring his mother back to life. Unfortunately Carl does not possess this power but however he has the ability to do and create other things.

"What are the five other rules? But also what else can you do with god's power"? Allen asked as he was curious and excited to know and witness what's about to happen next. "The other rules are I can't stop time, you can't commit genocide, I cannot die no matter what I try, and you can't leave the earth or destroy the earth. For example if I blow up the earth then this means I have left the earth. So therefore I would have then left the earth if I blew it up". Carl explains to Allen as he sits back in his chair taking another sip of patron out of the bottle.

"Holy fuck, so what else can you do with this power"? Allen asked and then he looked to his right and saw more beautiful naked women walking past them. "Everything else I can do and without any limits. This power allows me to have, to do and to become anything I want or think of". Carl explained as he hands the bottle of patron to Allen.

"That is awesome! Can you show me more of what you can do with god's power"? Allen said. "Let me ask you this, what would you like to do"? Allen paused for a few seconds and then it came to him. "I always wanted to know what it was like to fly. Not flying an air plane but actually fly like superman. I want to experience what it's like to fly and be free as a bird. Carl, show me how to fly". Allen asks with his hands open.

Without hesitation and without warning in one tenth of a second Allen and Carl were both thirty thousand feet in the air! Carl had his arms folded wearing a pair of sunglasses while they were hovering high in the air.

"Holy fuck"! Allen screamed while being in total shock as he realized how extremely high up in the air they were. "You wanted to know what it's like to fly. Well now here is your chance to fly like fucking superman"! Carl laughs at Allen for several reasons why. The main reason is because if Allen falls to his death, Carl can bring him back to life within a blink of an eye.

"Oh my god; how high up are we"? Allen asks "We are at thirty thousand feet". Carl replied. "I'm hovering we are hovering in the air". Allen says as he keeps looking down and all around him.

"Allen, are you ready? Are you ready to fly"? Carl asks "Fuck yeah I'm ready! But how do you fly? How does this work? Were floating right now above the clouds, but how do we fly"? Allen asked with excitement. Carl leans forward and says "I'll show you"!

Instantaneously Allen starts free falling heading towards the palace below them. As Allen is falling and screaming Carl appears right in front of him but standing straight up so it looks like they are upside down. "Are you having fun yet"? Carl says as he laughs at Allen watching him scream in horror.

"Help me I'm going to die"! Allen yells at Carl. Quickly Carl reaches out and touches Allen's head so he can transfer more power and knowledge to fly on his own. "Ok try it now! Allen, think and use your mind to fly. Trust me just use your thoughts and it will work"! Carl yells out loud so Allen can hear him.

"I can't do it I'm going to die"! Allen screams out! "You're not going to die. I won't let you die

Just listen to me, use your thoughts to control your movement. All you have to do is think, that's how it works". Carl responds back and instructing Allen on what to do.

Allen finally listened to Carl and now had full control. He shot straight up traveling faster than when he was falling to the ground. "There you go now you got it. Keep going now you can fly". Carl was happy and impressed watching his friend fly on his own.

As Carl watched this speeding bullet traveling faster and faster he then realized. this is not a good thing! Allen was getting to close to the earth's atmosphere. Then Carl cried out. "Allen, don't leave the earth"! Carl screamed in fear.

"This is fucking awesome"! Allen yelled out in complete joy and happiness. However it was too late and the speed Allen was traveling sent him far outside of the planet. Carl screamed no when he hit the invisible shield keeping him from leaving the planet. Carl could see his friend gasping for air to breathe. However instead of panicking, Carl focused his power on bringing Allen back inside the earth's atmosphere. Of course this only took half a second and he brought Allen back inside the atmosphere on the earth by using teleportation. Thank god it did not take Allen that long to catch his breath.

"How do you feel? I told you I won't let you die". Carl said as he was grateful to see his friend was still alive. "Holy fuck man, that was intense! Thank you for bringing me back". Allen says "No problem. Do you feel alright"? Carl asked with concern in his voice. "Carl I'm fine and I'm alive. Not only am I alive but I'm still hovering thousands of feet in the air"! Allen said as he was excited to fly around some more.

"So this means you're ready"? Carl asked. "Fuck yes I'm ready"! Allen says. "Then follow me and I will show you the entire world". Carl replies back.

Allen and Carl flew side by side heading towards the mountains of Canada. They were traveling at speeds of 1,200 MPH but once Carl and Allen reached the woods both of them lowered their speed to 50 MPH. This would allow them to maneuver around the trees, rocks and other obstacles in their way.

Carefully they fly through the woods in the mountains and dodging everything in their way with quick reflexes. Carl was impressed with Allen because he made it look like he had been flying for years.

"I told you it was easy. All you have to do is use your thoughts and you can fly better than any bird on this planet". Carl said to Allen as they flew together up the mountain. "Fuck yes! God I love it and I always wanted to do this"! Allen yells out with a feeling of high powered positive energy!

Carl lands on a boulder at the top of the mountain and Allen flies over the mountain but looks behind him and sees Carl lighting up a joint. Quickly Allen flew back to where Carl was standing and joined him for a smoke break.

"So what do you think so far"? Carl asks. "This is fucking incredible! Thank you, thank you for this Carl. I can never thank you enough for giving me this gift". Allen says with intense happiness on his face. "Don't worry about it Allen. I remember many years ago when you were there for me when I lost my foster parents and had to move again". Carl says as he passes the joint to Allen.

"I know and I remember how hard it was for you to lose your foster parents. You and I went through a lot of fucked up shit in our lives". Allen said after he took a long drag from his joint. "Yeah, we both have been through a lot of loss and pain". Carl said as he lit up another joint so Allen could have his.

"By the way how the fuck did you find me"? Allen asked Carl after he exhaled the marijuana smoke. "Remember I hold god's power. This means I knew exactly where you were. But let me ask you this, where in this world do you want to fly to next"? Carl asked. "This time follow me and keep up. Just let me know when you're ready". Carl takes a big drag from his joint and says "I'm ready, let's do this"!

With the sound of a sonic blast Allen took off faster than you can blink. However Carl stood behind still smoking his joint because he knew exactly where Allen was going. This is one of the many benefits to possessing the power of unlimited knowledge!

Without any quickness Carl casually closes his eyes. Once again Carl uses teleportation to appear in front of Allen but at the same time flying backwards. This freaked out Allen and scared him a bit because he was not expecting this. However Allen reminds himself of the awesome power Carl has. With a smile and a pair of sun glasses on Carl's face he says "Where to captain"? "Just follow me and I'll show you". Allen said but Carl already knew where Allen was headed.

They flew across the Atlantic and all the way to the island of Bali in Indonesia. Not only did Carl give Allen the ability to fly. He also gave him the power to fly at a top speed of 10,000 MPH. Even though Allen does not realize how fast he can actually fly but he is now living his dream. The dream of being able to fly goes all the way back to when Allen was a little kid. This will never be physically possible for any human being to fly without machines like air planes and helicopters. But with Carl's help Allen's childhood dream has now become a reality!

Allen was the first to land on the beautiful beach of Nusa Dua in Bali. Carl appeared sitting on a beach chair next to three palm trees. Allen looks back Carl and says "Fuck man, we are in paradise! I have always wanted to come here and I've always dreamed about this place"! Allen says with his arms and hands up in the air. A giant grin is on his face filled with joy and happiness.

"I'm glad you're happy Allen". Carl says as he claps his hands while laying back in his recliner. "I know what will make this place a better paradise". Carl says and then he claps his hands twice.

Beautiful women from all around the world, mini bars, luxury beds, a DJ playing all kinds of music and a massage table appeared out of thin air. "Now this is living the high life in paradise". Carl cried out loud! "Fuck yes! Yes! Thank you Carl, my god I've died and gone to heaven". Allen yelled out with an electrified excitement!

Carl was happy to spend this once in a life time chance with an old childhood friend. Because he knew when his time was up and the gift of god's power was gone. Allen would never know Carl. All of the memories they had, the great times they shared will all be gone. The only thing that is left will be the memories and the knowledge from the past.

Carl and Allen were having a fucking blast. With ice cold drinks in their hands, beautiful women who catered to their every need, perfect weather with no insects to bother them and every single drug in the world to have fun with. However Carl made sure Allen wasn't snorting too much cocaine. He did not want his friend overdosing.

Carl and Allen spent the week in all of the beaches of Bali. After they were done living a dream come true they set out on more adventures for a more few weeks.

Carl gives Allen a fortune of a hundred million dollars and the knowledge to invest the money so he will forever be financially secure. Before the last days are over with god's power Carl wanted to make sure his friend was financially taken care of.

Chapter 13

Seven days before the year will end and the gift is gone for Carl Smith. This man has been through and done so much for the world. Carl is the only one who was chosen to have this power and used it to help others across the planet. While the others became too obsessed with themselves they used this power for their selfish greed.

He unlocked the potential to travel through the cosmos in his spiritual form and learn how to see into the future by becoming the future itself. Of course this was not easy by any means because as you have seen Carl had to battle his way to get the answer. That battle became more like a new war of the worlds. But the goddess taught Carl what he needed to know.

This man created heaven on earth by becoming the earth and everything in and on the earth. There would be no more wars. Nobody stole from each other. People helped one another. Pollution did not exist anymore even though we still used gas and other forms of fuel. Humans stopped committing suicide and most of all there were no more wars. Militaries still existed for defense purposes in order to keep the peace.

Even before Carl created heaven on earth. He used his power to help cure the sick and the vulnerable. Carl cured a little boy named Michael and asked nothing in return other than a simple thank you.

Smith learned many things along his journey. The goddess known as mother taught him so much. She gave Carl her ultimate gift, the greatest power of all that she possesses the power of infinite knowledge and the answers to everything.

Carl visited an old and true friend. They both had the time of their lives and caught up talking about the old times. Most of all Carl Smith gave Allen a gift and the reality to live a childhood dream. Allen's dream was to fly without wings and to fly with complete control. The dream was also to have absolute freedom.

Carl used this power and his own imagination to not only have fun but to do things he always wanted to do. It is an incredible feeling knowing you can get away with anything and without any consequences. However, for the most part Carl used his abilities for the greater good of planet earth. Not to destroy the world or enslave the living on this planet.

Chapter 14

Mr. Smith wakes up in a 2,500 square foot bedroom on the fourth floor created and made by his own thoughts and ideas. On this extra king size bed was a lady built to perfection on each side of Carl. When Mr. Smith woke up so did these two beautiful women. They helped Carl out of bed to stretch and walk Carl out to the balcony.

All three of them were naked as they walked out to the balcony made of expensive stone. At the end of this balcony was a toilet made of pure silver with the seat up. Carl had this balcony customized they way he wanted.

You could see a beautiful landscape and the ocean as you look outwards from the balcony. Seeing the sun rising from the horizon at dead center from this balcony gave Mr. Smith a sense of perfection. Even though in my opinion perfection does not exist, it's always good to try your best!

One sexy lady holds Carl's dick so he can take the first piss of the day. While the other hands him a triple shot of espresso in a cup. "Thank you beautiful". Carl says to the sexy lady on his left. Meanwhile Mr. Smith takes a sip from his cup and in his right hand Carl is holding a foot long blunt.

"Can I light your blunt for you sir"? The lady says to Carl. "There's no need. But thank you for being so thoughtful sweetheart". Carl says to the young lady as he fires up his blunt instantaneously without using a lighter or a match. As this was going on the lady to Carl's right was still holding his dick while Carl kept taking his good morning piss.

A team of the sexy ladies were waiting in the shower for Carl to clean him up. After Carl was done taking the first piss of the day he finished his blunt within only two drags. With a quick though Mr. Smith used teleportation and appeared inside the shower. When Carl arrived in the shower all the girls were smiling and excited to see him. All the while Carl was still drinking his espresso because he magically refilled it.

After Carl was done taking his royal shower with the girls he was ready to start the day. Casually Carl walks out to the back yard towards the Olympic size pool. He sees the back of a man's head as he sat inside Carl's gazebo.

Mr. Smith didn't have to worry about a fucking thing. Remember Carl earned the power of knowledge and the answers to everything. So Carl is now officially Mr. knows it all!

Carl walks around the gazebo to the entrance and sees Joseph sitting in the center of the gazebo with a drink in his hand. Joseph also has a German blond lady sucking his dick. At the same time another lady from Japan had pouch of Joseph's favorite tobacco. The Japanese lady was also packing Joseph's pipe. This one was different than the other pipe Joseph had.

"Well hello Car. How's your morning going so far? Also would you care for drink"? Joseph offered Carl. "Yes I would Joseph but it looks your busy over there". Carl said. "Oh no need to worry kid this young lady is almost done".

Twenty seconds later, Mr. Joseph released and sprayed his liquid children straight this kind girl's esophagus and into her stomach. This definitely made Joseph feel relaxed and ready to take on the world!

"Why thank you darling you did an amazing job"! Joseph said to her as she helped pull his pants up. Meanwhile that same bottle from the interview appeared on the gazebo.

"Can I get you anything"? Carl asks as Joseph lights his pipe while the Japanese lady gives him a shoulder massage. "No thank you Carl, I'm doing just fine". Joseph says after he exhales the smoke.

"So tell me something kid have you been enjoying yourself with the gift we have given you? By the way you have done an excellent job with god's power. Do you have any plans or a thought when you're time is up and the gift is gone"? Joseph asked Carl. "I have a few". Carl responds as he sits down next to Joseph.

"Carl we are all very proud of your accomplishments. It's never easy battling the goddess of Mother Nature. She definitely is unique in different ways". Joseph says as Carl pours himself a drink. "I miss her already. But I have a feeling that I will see her again.

Joseph took a drag from his pipe and smiled at Carl. He paused for three seconds and he said this. "My dear boy you already know the answer to that question. Remember you are now officially Mr. knows it all". Joseph then hands Carl a drink and they toast to each other.

"By the way Carl do you still have the infinite card"? Joseph asks. "I sure do". Carl replies back. "May I please have it"? Joseph asks as he holds out his left hand. "No problem". And then Carl hands over the infinite card.

"The infinite card never held any power at all". Carl said as Joseph held the car in one hand and a deck of cards in the other. "You are smart Carl. And you yes you are correct. It's just a card and only a card. The universe is what gave you and the others this power". Joseph explains while a grin forms on Carl's face.

"So what would you like to do since you're here old man? That's right, let's relax and enjoy this moment in time". Carl says. "You got it rookie. You already know the future". Joseph says as he raises his glass and starts laughing.

"Son of a fucking bitch, you and the entire universe handpicked me on purpose! You all knew this entire time. I would be the one to create heaven on earth. To go beyond my physical form and into the spiritual body by using DMT. Not only that but to battle the goddess in order to see the future by becoming the future"! Carl says with a look of shock and understanding on his face.

"Where so many failed and abused this power. I was the one you were all waiting for. The one who could survive successfully after my time was up and the power was gone. Not only that but if did fail there would be more to come. As long as the human race keeps going there would always be a chance to achieve what I have accomplished". Carl says as he refills his glass.

"Bingo kid. Are you having fun yet"? Joseph laughs as he raises his glass in the air. This was the moment he has been waiting for!

Chapter 15

The morning came when the gift was over and the power was gone. The only true power left for Carl was his memory. Inside Carl's memories was the power of unlimited knowledge and the answers to everything across the universe!

Carl smith was reborn again into this world and a new beginning has begun for and the rest of the planet. Where exactly did Carl wake up at? What part of the world was he in? Mr. knows it all woke up on a kitchen floor. Not just any Kitchen floor but on the kitchen floor inside the white house in Washington DC.

I'm guessing you weren't expecting this to happen. But guess who did other than me. That's right Carl knew exactly where he was going to wake up at. He was happy and grateful about waking up inside the white house.

Carl was naked, tired, and hungry. At the same time filled with joy. Nobody else was in the kitchen, Carl was the only one. However it did not take long for the secret service to run into the kitchen with their guns aimed at Carl.

"Get your fucking hands in the air right now! Don't you fucking move! How did you get here"? One of the secret services agents asked. "Good morning Mike, Dan, Joe, Aaron, James and John. How are you guys doing today"? Carl said in a calm voice with his hands up.

All six secret service agents had shocking looks on their faces! Meanwhile Carl had a smile on his face and showing no fear. "Who are you and how did you get here"? The secret service agent yelled at Carl. "Guys if you can please get some clothes to wear. I will gladly tell you what's going".

The secret service escorted Carl to a secure room and gave him a brand new suit, tie, with dress shoes and socks to wear. Carl looked liked a successful business man.

"Gentlemen you're probably not going to believe this but I am from the future. I'm a time traveler from the year 2185. I know it's hard to believe but I can prove it to you guys. I have all the time in the world"!

Six of the secret service agents looked at Carl with disbelief. However one of the agents named James said to the other five. "Well this guy appeared out of thin air. Let's find out if he really is telling the truth or not".

To be continued...

Made in the USA
Columbia, SC
23 November 2022